Grab

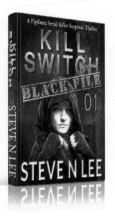

You get *Black File 01* free with this book (see Table of Contents for details).

Kill Switch

Angel of Darkness Book 01

Steve N. Lee

Copyright

Kill Switch

Chapter 01

LIKE PLAYING RUSSIAN roulette in slow motion, waiting for death tortured Catalina. Even though she had accepted the end was coming, she could still do nothing but wait for it to creep up and surprise her one day. Her mom joked it was God's worst ever practical joke. Cat wished *she* could be so lighthearted about it too.

To shield herself from the rain, Cat held her tourist map of Krakow over her head as she scurried across the cobbled square dotted with bedraggled pedestrians.

Town Hall Tower loomed over her. Yesterday in the sun, the two-hundred-foot Gothic structure had looked majestic with its arched windows, stone lions guarding its entrance, and warm, cream-colored stone contrasted with red brick. Reminding her of home, the architecture had given her a welcome glow.

Today, with storm clouds sitting on its spire, the shadowy tower oozed foreboding. And that made her ache for home so much it hurt. Except, after what she'd done, there was no place she could call home.

Her rain-drenched canvas shoes squelching, Cat tramped down yet another narrow street of dull red, blue and gray medieval buildings. Four days ago, she'd had a home, a career, a future. Then they'd traveled here and become all but destitute. Hell, she hated this city for what it had done to her and her mom.

Goddamnit, she couldn't think like that. She had to stay strong. After all, she wasn't the one dying. Though that would make it a million times easier. No, it was her mom – the only person in the world who 'got' her.

In an antique store window, Cat glimpsed a gold-framed mirror.

She cringed. "Oh, God."

Her eyes were puffy from all her crying. Her usually flowing brown hair hung a straggly mess. And with all the stress and sleepless nights, her skin... As gray and lifeless as the cobbled streets. Hell, she looked a haggard forty-seven, not a vibrant twenty-seven.

She huffed. Her cosmetics had gone along with everything else. Everything. Their entire world had been packed into that car.

She trudged into yet another hotel. In a walnut-paneled lobby, red armchairs sat before a stone fireplace with a crest chiseled into the chimney breast depicting three castle towers above an eagle.

Cat looked down at her clothes. Utterly soaked, her white cotton top clung to her breasts as if she'd come to audition for a porn movie. Great.

She bumped into someone.

A woman glanced up from texting, blond hair cascading over her shoulders and red lips pouting like in some cheap fashion magazine.

Coming as second nature, Cat apologized. "Imi pare rau." Oh, damn, she had to remember to speak Polish, not Romanian. "Um... Przepraszam."

The woman winced a smile and strutted toward the exit.

At the reception desk ahead, a sullen woman with her hair in a bun stared at an LCD monitor.

Cat drew a deep breath, then strode forward, shoulders back, head up, trying to shake off all the earlier rejections. In her mind, she rehearsed the Polish speech her mom had prepared, but with each step, her pounding heart battered the words, making them harder and harder to pronounce.

The receptionist smiled at Cat with all the warmth of a fishmonger looking at a dead cod. In Polish, she said, "Hello."

Cat replied in Polish, "Hi, do you, uh... uh... have any work, please? I'm – I'm, um, willing to do anything."

All Cat needed was just enough to pay their extra costs while they waited to see if the police recovered their car. It wasn't like she was asking for charity. Hell, no. Just a chance.

"No, sorry." The woman returned to her monitor without another word.

"Thank you." Cat squeezed out a smile and then slouched away.

That was the ninth rejection that morning and the thirty-sixth in all. But she couldn't give up. Staying here was eating into the money they'd scraped together. If she didn't replace it, they'd never get to England. And they had to get there. Had to. If her mom didn't receive the treatment she needed... Hell, Cat would sell her goddamn soul to get the money if she had to.

A café sat across the street, decorated with cheerful greens and yellows, its sidewalk tables empty because of the rain. She tramped over.

Inside, the aroma of fresh pastries enveloped Cat. A chubby guy waltzed past her carrying a plate piled with enough delicacies to feed a family, crumbs on his lips from the bite he'd already taken.

Cat's mouth watered. Having had no breakfast, she yearned to splurge, but knew she'd hate herself afterward for wasting money. Trying not to look at any food, she joined the line behind a skinny guy sending a tweet.

As the line dwindled, Cat reached into her canvas purse and gently held her four-leaf clover in its plastic pouch. She had a good feeling about this place. Yes, this was the place where she saved her mom.

At the counter, she spoke Polish to a middle-aged woman with a strawberry-shaped nose.

"Hi, do you have any work, please? I, uh, I'm willing to do anything."

"Yes," said the woman.

Cat gasped. "Yes?"

But then the woman spouted more Polish at her.

Cat caught a couple of words she understood, but they meant nothing out of context. She gawked wide-eyed.

The woman frowned, then repeated what she'd said.

Cat swallowed hard. "Um..." They'd only had time for her mom to prep her on a handful of phrases. After all, how much Polish did she need to wash dishes or mop floors?

A bead of sweat trickled from Cat's temple. She looked at the nearby customers, hoping someone might somehow come to her rescue. A girl chewed gum, staring at her phone; an old lady rooted in her pink purse; a handsome man in a suit caught her eye but looked away.

Her heart hammering, she grabbed the only chance she had – she asked if the woman spoke English. "Czy mowi pani po angielsku?"

The woman waved Cat away and went back to her work.

No! Cat needed this job. She called out, "Anything. Please."

The woman shook her head without even looking up.

Cat tottered toward the exit, feeling like she'd been sucker punched. She'd had a chance. And then blown it. How was she going tell her mom?

Wobbly from the unending upset, she rested a hand on the table near the door to steady herself. Her breath shuddered as she struggled to control her emotions. She failed. As if someone were balling it like a sheet of paper, Cat's face scrunched up and tears rolled down her cheeks.

Something brushed her hand on the table, so she glanced down.

The texting blonde from the hotel had pushed a napkin across to her.

Cat nodded her thanks, then dabbed her eyes.

With a sigh, she gazed out into the unforgiving rain, then shuffled outside. She peered along the street for other opportunities. Okay, so who was going to make her feel like crap next?

Behind her, someone spoke in English. "Miss?"

Cat ignored them, it never registering that someone was actually talking to her.

A hand touched her shoulder. She jumped and whipped around.

Beneath a black umbrella, a man with wavy brown hair and gentle blue eyes smiled at her – the handsome man in the suit from the café.

He said, "You look for job?"

"Yes. Why?"

He held his arms wide. "I cleaner job have." The rain momentarily fell onto his navy suit, which had obviously been tailored for him.

After all the rejection, she was unsure whether he was being kind or playing a cruel joke. "A cleaning job for me? Really?"

"We are charity, so is small money, but for you, really, I have job." He handed her a business card with the name embossed in gold. "Jacek Grabowski."

"Catalina Petrescu." Beaming, she shook his hand. "Thank you. Thank you so much."

"You welcome." He smiled warmly. "You Hungarian? Czech?"

"Romanian."

"Oh, Romanians wonderful people. Very wonderful."

He held his umbrella out to share it. "Please."

Cat grinned. He had manners and work, and could speak a language she understood. After all the bad luck they'd suffered, finally, some good luck had come their way. And thank God – that man from their consulate hadn't yet returned her call and they were burning through their money fast.

As she ducked under his umbrella, knocking came from the café. She peeped around him.

The blonde woman rapped on the window. When she caught Cat's eye, she shook her head vigorously. Cat checked over her shoulder to see if the blonde was gesturing to someone behind her. She wasn't. How odd. It was almost as if the blonde thought something was wrong, as if she felt she had to warn Cat.

Jacek lightly touched Cat's arm to draw her attention back to him and smiled. "You want see job?"

Chapter 02

WHEN CAT DIDN'T immediately reply to his offer, Jacek said, "If no, is okay."

Cat wasn't sure what to say now. Such an offer was almost too good to be true. Especially when she didn't know anything about this man. But she needed money to get her mom to England, to get her the treatment she needed, to get the chance to enjoy a few more months together, maybe even years. Could she really say No?

Could she say No? Wasn't the real question, could she say Yes?

If she went, maybe, there was a chance she'd earn the money to have a few more months with her mother, but there was an even bigger chance she'd end up bruised and bloodied in some dark alley. How dumb would she have to be to go somewhere with some strange guy she'd just met on the street?

"Thanks" – she grimaced and reached to hand the business card back – "but I can't."

Jacek held his free hand up defensively. "Don't tell me, don't tell me. Strange man in strange country is offering strange job and you afraid all is not good, yes?"

"Sorry, but…" Her cheeks burned with the embarrassment of having implied a helpful stranger was probably little more than a cunning rapist.

He laid a hand on her arm so gently he barely touched her. "Please, is no reason be sorry. If I you, I no trust this 'strange man' either." He wagged a finger at her. "Is good to be so questioning. Is easier be safe."

She forced a feeble smile, feeling her cheeks cooling with his understanding.

"So," he said, taking his smartphone from his pocket, "let me prove you all is good."

He swiped this way and that on the huge screen, then handed the device to her.

"Is website: Krakow Wellness Center." He gestured to the screen. "You look."

The image on the website's home page showed a modern two-storey concrete building, its windows gleaming in the sunshine. It looked the type of place she'd always dreamed of working.

He craned his neck to see the screen in her hand and pointed to the dropdown menu. "Please to click."

Cat did so. The menu gave various options in Polish, none of which meant anything to her.

"Please to click O Nas. It means… er… what it means in English? Ah, yes, About Us."

Cat nodded and clicked as instructed. Another page opened.

Jacek said, "And we are scrolling."

Cat scrolled down over paragraphs of text.

Jacek prompted her to continue. "And we are scrolling. And we are scrolling."

Finally, another image appeared. An image of a man in a tailored suit.

Jacek said, "Ta da!" He proudly held his arms wide again.

Cat smiled. "It's you!"

"And what it is saying under photo, please?"

Even though it was in Polish, there was no mistaking the meaning. A wave of relief swept over Cat.

She looked up at him and beamed. "Dyrektor."

He bowed his head. "Jacek Grabowski. At your service."

Cat grinned. This guy wasn't only genuine, but the head of an entire medical facility. If he said there was work, there was work. Guaranteed.

A warm glow welled up from inside her. She'd done it. She'd found a way to get the money to save her mom.

Taking his phone back, Jacek said, "Now, please say you do job because it is big emergency we are having."

"Emergency?"

He sucked through his teeth. "Oh, very, very big. To be very true, is not me helping you, but you helping me."

"Why? What happened?"

"Fire. Small, but smoke is ruin so much." He shook his head. "Is mess everywhere. Is patients everywhere. Is problems, problems, problems. Everywhere."

"So you want temporary workers to help you clean up the mess?"

"Exactly."

It was ideal. Easy money. No commitment. Just what she needed.

He must have seen the relief in her expression.

"So, you want job? Yes?"

"Yes. Yes, I want it. Thank you. Thank you so much."

"Ah, wonderful. So come" – he gestured down the street – "I have car."

Cat shrank back. "Car? Right now?"

"Is problem?"

Okay, so she now knew who this guy was and where he was supposed to be taking her, but no one else knew that.

He smiled and nodded. "You very, very careful person. Is good."

"I just need twenty minutes to go and tell my mom."

He frowned. "You not have phone?"

"It won't work in Poland."

"Ahhh. Please." He held out a different phone – a lump of gray plastic with a tiny screen. "This cheaper for local calling. Now, phone friend, phone mother, phone father. Phone all. Tell you safe with Jacek Grabowski here." He pointed to the address on his card in her hand.

"Oh, thank you. I'll be as quick as I can."

Her phone didn't work, but her mom's did because it was on a different network. Cat called and broke the news, her eyes filling up as she explained how everything was now going to be okay. And before her mom became concerned that her daughter was going somewhere with a man she'd only just met, Cat gave Jacek's name and details of the center, including the website address.

She smiled at Jacek, who smiled back, but then looked at his gold watch.

Not wanting to upset her new employer, Cat said she'd phone again in a couple of hours to say how everything was going, then ended the call.

"Is good?" Jacek said, taking his phone back.

"Fantastic."

"Okay cokey, then we go."

They set off. As he passed a round green trash can, Jacek nonchalantly tossed something in. Cat didn't see what, but it clanged as it hit the metal side.

Minutes later, while chatting, Cat looked out of the car window as they cruised through rain-drenched backstreets. Gone were the hordes of tourists and the magnificent architecture. Here, people trudged along as if the air was heavier and squashed them into the ground, while the buildings were so gray, they looked like the rain had washed all the color out of them.

Finally, Jacek parked outside a gigantic four-story slab of concrete. Car-sized graffiti tags plastered the building's walls, smashed windows bled darkness, and patches of the exterior crumbled to the ground.

"This where is my addict charity." He pointed to a doorway in the middle, next to a derelict store plastered with flyers.

Cat's stomach clenched. Where was the modern building with the gleaming windows?

"Here?" She gazed up at the grimy monstrosity.

"This temporary place for emergency. I say you about fire. About patients everywhere. Remember?"

"Yes, but…"

"So we must to move some patients here. For temporary. We buy this place but is big repair so is very long job."

She said, "You've been renovating it?" That explained the state of the place.

"Sorry?"

"Renovating – repairing, building again."

"Ah, thank you. Yes, is big renovating. But one day, will be big beautiful like other building."

Cat nodded, though she couldn't imagine it from the state of the place today.

"Come," he said, clambering out. "I show job."

Cat drew a deep breath. She didn't like the change of venue, but surely that was just her being overly cautious. After all, she'd given her mom details of everything. What kind of rapist would let his victim pass on his name, phone number, employment details, and even a website featuring his photo? If anything untoward happened, it wasn't like the police would put anyone else at the top of their list of suspects.

No, she was worrying over nothing. God, she could be so dumb sometimes. This was her chance. Maybe her last. She would not lose it.

Cat got out of the car. "How many women are you helping now?"

"Um… for drink maybe five. For drug, I think three."

After he spoke into an intercom, the door unlocked. He ushered her into a corridor. Ahead, a staircase doubled back on itself, so she couldn't see the upper floor. Rock music drifted down from upstairs.

"You see – to clean," said Jacek.

He pointed to the carpet of brown swirls. It was so dirty it was hard to tell where the pattern ended and the filth began.

"Uh-huh." Though burning would be a better option.

"To clean." He waved at a mottled black patch on the wall.

As they ascended the stairs, a stench like a men's locker room greeted Cat. At the top, a shaven-headed man lounged at a reception desk watching music videos on a laptop. Another man sprawled over a green sofa with a pizza box resting on his immense belly.

Anxious, but wanting to be friendly, Cat smiled. "Hello."

No one replied.

Jacek guided her into a hallway where discolored paint peeled off the walls due to damp. Along either side were five treatment rooms. All the doors were closed except the two at the far end. Cat thanked God she wasn't a patient here with such awful accommodation and unfriendly staff. Still, if you had an addiction, poor help was better than no help.

Whimpering came from behind the second door on the right, like a tiny girl crying herself to sleep. Except, the tone of voice suggested it was not a child. A junkie suffering withdrawals, maybe.

Jacek entered the last room on the left and flipped the light switch. Under a low wattage bulb, the room hung in gloom.

"So maybe you clean and if good, is job yours. Yes?"

Cat gawked at bedding so stained it looked like someone had emptied a pot of goulash over it, a sink caked in grime, and a carpet so dirty she couldn't tell its original color.

"Great." Nothing would stop her making the money to save her mom.

"Okay cokey. Then—"

A gruff voice thundered down the hall.

"Oh, is Artur, big boss," said Jacek. "I must to go."

He left, shutting the door behind him.

Cat heaved a breath. She'd wanted work, but so much of it? She tramped to the closet to look for cleaning supplies, but it was empty. Neither were there any under the sink or the bed. Okay, she'd ask Jacek.

She marched to the door and reached to open it, but stopped dead.

There was no handle.

Chapter 03

CAT CHECKED THE floor to see if the handle had dropped off. No. What the…?

Clawing her fingertips into the tiny gap between the door and the frame, she pulled. The door didn't budge.

She braced herself. Heaved.

Her right index fingernail broke low down. She cursed, then sucked her fingertip.

Now what? She'd feel like a fool if she called for help only to find there was a knack to opening the door she'd been too stupid to spot.

She heaved again.

It was shut tight.

She knocked on the door. "Jacek, I'm sorry, but the door is stuck."

No answer.

Okay, this was getting a little weird now. She glanced around at the room. The hairs stood on the back of her neck at being trapped in here much longer.

"Jacek." She called louder. "Jacek, I'm stuck."

Nothing.

Her heart pounded and she felt giddy as adrenaline surged through her body. She wanted to get out of here. She needed to get out of here.

Cat hammered her fist on the door. "Jacek!"

Even if he'd left, there were at least two other men. Why was no one helping?

She banged harder. Shouted louder. "Help. Please. Help."

Finally, footsteps pounded down the hall. A gruff voice muttered in Polish.

She heard the handle at the other side turn. The door swung open.

A stocky man glowered at her. With wiry red hair and stubble on a weather-beaten face, he looked like an old seadog.

It wasn't her fault she'd gotten trapped, but if he was the 'big boss', she better apologize to ensure she kept this job.

"I'm very sorry, but the door—"

His fist smashed into her face.

She crashed over backwards, cracking her head against the floor.

On her back, she stared up. Tiny lights twinkled in her blurred vision.

For a moment, she couldn't think where she was or what had happened. The lights faded and the place came into focus. She tried to push up, but her arms gave and she fell back. As if she was drunk, the room spun and sounds slurred.

Her head so fuzzy, like a bystander, she watched the shaven-headed guy and the one with the huge belly grab her by the arms. They hauled her up.

In Romanian, she said, "Thank you." Unsteady on her feet, she clutched the two men holding her and said, "Sorry, I'll be okay. Just give me a minute."

They held her suspended. Seadog grabbed her chin and twisted her head about, studying her.

The fog in her mind started to clear. Someone had punched her. Why? She hadn't locked the damned door.

Seadog said something in Polish, then mauled her left breast.

With her arms pinned, all she could do was twist to try to stop him.

He slammed a fist into her gut.

She slumped forward, wheezing. Pain exploded in her stomach as if she'd been shot.

What was happening? Why were they doing this? Questions whirled in her mind.

She stared at the door. The open door. Pushing with all the might in her legs and arms, she made a run for it.

But they had her fast and clawed her back.

Seadog barked more Polish. The men holding her threw her onto the bed. Shaven Head grabbed her wrists and stretched out her arms over her head; his friend grabbed her ankles and pulled her legs out straight.

She kicked. A foot cracked the fat guy in the face.

Seadog hammered his fist into her midriff again.

The strike knocked the wind out of her. Her mouth opened, her lungs strained, her body cried out for air, but she couldn't breathe. A high-pitched croaking sound was all that came out.

Then she felt it. And knew her nightmare had only just begun.

Seadog's hand disappeared under her skirt. He grabbed her underwear. Yanked. Threw the torn white cotton panties across the room.

Rough fingers prodded and poked.

She flinched as coarse hands scraped over her delicate flesh like sandpaper.

Finally, Cat gasped a great breath. Energy surged through her once more.

She squirmed.

Twisted.

Jerked.

Her voice breaking, she said, "No, please. Don't. Please."

But Seadog clasped his hand around her throat and squeezed.

Once again fighting for breath, she could hardly move.

He climbed on top of her.

Oh God, no. Please. No. This couldn't be happening. No, this happened to other women. Not to her. Please God, not to her.

She couldn't see what he was doing, but she knew from the way he was moving – unfastening his trousers.

Tears ran down the sides of Cat's head while she gagged and spluttered for air.

His rough fingers poked at her crotch again. Then something else prodded there.

Her stomach churned, her innards heaving like someone had reached down her throat to drag them out. If she'd had anything to eat that day, she'd have hurled it all over herself.

She twisted her hips. Struggled to rip her arms free. Struggled to kick out. Struggled to break free. But she could barely move.

Then...

Oh, God, he was in her. He was in her. HE WAS IN HER!

Chapter 04

IN THE BAR, Tess cradled a bottle of beer while sitting with her back to the wall so she could see the restroom doors, and the front and rear exits. She'd picked up this awareness technique in Shanghai from Sergei, her ex-Spetsnaz lover, who'd taught her the finer points of handling a gun. He'd always insisted on sitting in a spot from where he could see everyone's comings and goings so no one could sneak up on him. Awareness had become a key element in Tess's combat strategies.

Sergei would've liked this bar – black wooden beams from a bygone age, a wall of majestic crests emblazoned with castles and lions and warriors, and ale strong enough to stand a spoon in. It was how she'd always pictured the Russian bars he reminisced about.

She took another sip of beer and watched a group of boisterous young men walk in. Automatically, she scanned each one, deciding how she'd put them down if she had cause to – break the fat one's knee, gouge the small one's eye, punch the tall one in the throat, and, hey what the hell, just go crazy and have fun with the last one.

Awareness again. When violence was such a big part of her life, she had to be constantly aware of her environment, and who and what filled it. Unless she'd lost interest in breathing.

But she hadn't been looking for trouble tonight. No, all she'd wanted was a quiet drink at the end of a busy day. However, just because she wasn't looking for trouble didn't mean she wouldn't find it. Especially when the couple next to her were just begging for it.

At the next table, a young couple coiled around each other like mating snakes. In between dental inspections with their tongues, they swigged the occasional mouthful of beer and chatted in English – he fluently; she with a struggle. Tess had singled them out the moment the guy had opened his mouth and spoken to his Polish girlfriend. Yes, they couldn't have made better targets if they'd painted bull's-eyes on their backs.

From Tess's eavesdropping, she guessed he was early twenties, but because of his baby face, she'd bet he had to regularly produce ID in bars back home.

His girlfriend was even slimmer than Tess. Yet had bigger breasts. Much bigger. In fact, too big. In Tess's vainer moments, she dreamed of going up a cup size to a C, but this girl? Hell, if Tess had boobs that size she'd marry the first chiropractor she came across.

The boyfriend stood up. "Come on."

He pulled his girlfriend by the hand to drag her out of her seat, but she stayed put.

She spoke with an accent as thick as she was pretty, "One beer more."

Her sentence sounded awkward and slow, as if the words really shouldn't be anywhere near each other. It was always the same for Tess when she learned a new language – she always came off sounding like a broken robot. And it never got any easier, no matter how many languages she learned. Maybe if she did it for the love of learning, it would be different. But that wasn't the case. She'd had no choice but to learn to talk to people in their own language. It was the only way to acquire the tools she needed to do what she had to do when she finally made it back to the States.

The boyfriend tried again. "Come on. We can come here again tomorrow." He tugged gently on her arm.

"Is early."

"It's not. It's nearly half-one."

She shrugged as if she didn't understand and said something in Polish.

He showed her his watch.

She threw her arms up. "Is very early."

"Please." The word was long and drawn out, like a little boy begging his mom for another cookie.

She rolled her eyes, but then smirked at him. "Okay."

They meandered out arm-in-arm.

Tess waited a few moments, then followed.

Chapter 05

THE COUPLE SAUNTERED through the Old Town's main square, the sheen of rainwater on the cobbles glistening with the reflection of the street lights. They laughed and spoke pidgin English, often using phrases out of context which obviously meant something special only to them.

Tess hung in the shadowy arches of the Cloth Hall's colonnade. With her straight dark hair, black gloves, black jeans and black leather jacket, the darkness engulfed her with ease.

By day and well into the evening, the square pulsed with activity, most of it concentrated in the outdoor seating of the bars and restaurants that encircled the square and, to a lesser extent, around the Cloth Hall which sat in the square's center, a colonnade of nineteen arches down each of its sides.

At this time of the night, most family-oriented establishments had closed for the day, while the bars hidden up alleyways and secreted in the backs of buildings blazed into life for the city's party animals.

Tess waited. Her targets weren't in the optimum position for a strike yet. Maybe they never would be.

Unless the situation changed, she'd lurk out of sight. Hidden. A nobody. Doing nothing. Nowhere.

The couple ambled toward the end of the square, passing Saint Mary's Church, its two giant towers gazing down on them like world-weary gods.

Tess slunk through the colonnade, shrouded in darkness.

As the couple neared a narrow street leading away from the square, they argued playfully over which country produced the best beer. The boyfriend insisted it was his because they had more variety, while the girlfriend insisted it was hers because theirs were stronger.

Tess slipped out of the arches and followed them down Florianska Street, clinging to the shadows.

The designer stores and global food chains lay deserted and darkened. Ahead loomed the thirty-three-meter Gothic tower that was Saint Florian's Gate, guarding Krakow as part of the city walls as it had for centuries.

Carefree, the couple ambled down the sidewalk, while Tess lurked in the darkness in which she spent so much of her life. The couple seemed to be heading straight for the archway that sliced through the tower and led to the narrow park which surrounded the Old Town. But the archway didn't only lead to the park...

The Barbican. A perfect location for an attack.

Tess quickened her pace to move in as the couple passed through the arch.

At the other side of the archway, the Barbican lurked in the gloom. With seven turrets clawing the night sky, the circular structure had probably witnessed more bloodshed than any other part of the city, having showered invaders with arrows and molten tar.

Tess's heart pounded in anticipation and nervous energy surged through her body. She wiped her palms on her jeans, then balled her fists.

As the couple strolled along the path through the trees, a figure loomed out of hiding.

A stocky man in a motorcycle jacket shouted at them, "Hey, America."

The couple stopped. Turned.

Two young Polish men strutted towards them.

"America," said Motorcycle Jacket, "why you come here for Polish woman?"

His tall skinny friend shouted, "Because America women all hundred-kilo hamburger ass."

Motorcycle Jacket laughed and patted his friend on the back.

"Sorry," said the boyfriend, "but I'm not American; I'm English."

Motorcycle Jacket shrugged as if anything the boyfriend said wouldn't make any difference.

"England. America. All same – come to Poland, take our rich job, take our beautiful woman." He thumped his chest. "But Poland our country. Our!"

The girlfriend shouted something in Polish.

Two other men stepped from the park's tree line and blocked the path behind the couple. One of them, in a hoodie, shouted at her in Polish.

The boyfriend looked around, his gaze flying in all directions. He was obviously searching for an escape route. There wasn't one. He pulled his girlfriend behind him and backed away to the side of the path, bushes blocking any chance of them running.

The boyfriend's timid stare flashed from one threat to the next and back again. "Look, we don't want any trouble. Leave us alone, please."

"You no want trouble?" Motorcycle Jacket sneered and shook his head. "Then fuck off home, fucking America."

As Motorcycle Jacket swaggered over, the boyfriend put his hands up submissively. "Please. Just leave us alone."

Motorcycle Jacket pushed the boyfriend's arms aside and smacked him in the head with a haymaker.

The boyfriend fell and sprawled on the asphalt. In the dirt, he threw his arms up and cowered. "Please. Please, don't."

Motorcycle Jacket spat on him. "Fucking mommy boy."

He kicked the boyfriend in the gut.

The boyfriend screamed and hunched over, clutching his midriff.

Tess sprang from the darkness. She hammered a kick into the back of Motorcycle Jacket's knee. As he slumped backwards, she ripped him back by his hair and slammed the side of her fist down onto his collarbone, eliciting a satisfying crunch.

Motorcycle Jacket shrieked and clutched his broken bone with his left hand while his right arm hung useless at his side.

Frozen, the tall guy who'd been standing next to him stared wide-eyed.

Tess was never one to turn down a golden opportunity – she whipped out another kick. Her shin bit into his thigh, deadening the nerve, which took away his mobility to keep him an easy target.

33

She crashed in a flurry of punches ending with a massive right hook.

Two of the guy's teeth hit the asphalt path a fraction of a second before he did.

The guy in the hoodie ran at her, while his friend, a pudgy guy, hung back.

Tess waited for Hoodie. There was little point expending energy going to him when he was coming to her.

He heaved his right hand back and flung a giant of a haymaker at her.

Hoodie telegraphed his attack so clearly, Tess could have dealt with it blindfolded.

His fist thundered at her.

Confronted by explosive violence, the average person backed away, threw their arms up, or cowered to hide. And that was why the average person got the crap beaten out of them on the street.

Tess did not back away.

Did not shield herself.

Did not cower.

Instead, she moved closer to the danger.

She guided the punch harmlessly past with her left forearm while grabbing him around the back with her other hand.

She spun around.

Bent forward.

Flipped him over her hip.

Splattered him into the sidewalk.

Still holding his arm, Tess immobilized it in a figure-four armlock, then levered it that little bit further, bending what should never bend.

Hoodie cried out as his elbow cracked loudly.

Tess glared at the pudgy guy, the last of the four targets standing.

Backing off, he held up his open hands and spouted Polish.

Tess couldn't understand a word, but she understood the waver in his voice.

She took two bounds toward him, then stopped and watched him hightail it into the blackness.

She turned and glared at the three men she'd put on the ground. Warily, they each clambered to their feet, cradling their injuries.

Without saying a word, she strolled towards them.

They backed away. Not one able to fight.

With a nod of her head Tess motioned toward the archway back to the Old Town.

As quickly as they could, they lurched away, regularly glancing back to check where she was.

No, Tess hadn't been looking for trouble tonight. However, she hadn't exactly gone out of her way to avoid it. And it wasn't like she'd killed anyone. A few months of hospital treatment and they'd all be fine. Meanwhile, the streets would be a little safer. Plus, now that these goons knew what could be lurking in the shadows watching them, hunting innocent people for kicks might lose some of its appeal.

Tess turned to the couple who'd been ambushed.

Sitting on the ground, the boyfriend stared at her openmouthed, holding the side of his face where he'd been hit. His girlfriend clung to him, her fingers clawed into his shirt. They both flinched as Tess stepped toward them.

Finally, Tess spoke. "Are you two okay?"

The boyfriend stared. "Huh? Er... er... yeah. Er, thank you."

"You're welcome." Tess reached down a hand to him.

He looked warily into her eyes, as if not knowing whether he was going to be pulled to safety or have his shoulder wrenched out of its socket. After a second, he clasped her hand. She hauled him up.

Tess said, "You haven't heard about the gangs targeting English speakers who have Polish girlfriends?"

He shook his head, looking at her blankly. "We've only been in Krakow a couple of days."

"When are you leaving?"

"Tomorrow. After we've visited Auschwitz."

"That's probably wise. There are more of those assholes around."

"Okay."

"Hey, and don't go wasting your money booking a special tour to Auschwitz. It'll cost you five times more than just getting a local bus yourself."

"You've been?"

"No. Actually, I was planning on going tomorrow too. Anyway, can you make it back to your hotel okay?"

He pointed to the street on the other side of the Barbican. "It's only a minute or two."

"Good. But be careful."

"Yeah. And thanks again."

Tess watched them totter down the path, then turned to leave.

She shivered, though it was a warm evening. The fight was over, but something didn't feel quite right. A tingling sensation all but ate away her spine, the way it always did whenever something was wrong but she couldn't put her finger on it. Was someone watching her?

The bushes rustled behind her.

She spun around.

Pulled her fists up.

Scoured the shadows.

Nothing but blackness stared back at her.

Squinting to catch the tiniest of movements, Tess surveyed the clawing darkness.

Nothing.

Strange. Her instincts were rarely wrong.

She prowled along the path.

But the hair bristled on the back of her neck.

She stopped.

Peered into the shadows again.

This wasn't over. There was something wrong here. But what was it?

Chapter 06

AUSCHWITZ. THE NAME conjured all manner of nightmarish visions, yet few lived up to the real horrors unveiled to its visitors.

The spring sun blazed outside, but a deathly chill crawled up Tess's spine. Alone, she stood in the center of the room, enclosed by nothing but grungy concrete walls, a concrete floor, and a concrete ceiling. No windows. No furniture. No decoration. But why would there be? A gas chamber needed no such finery.

Enveloped by an eerie silence like that of a church crypt, she scanned the room.

The Nazis slaughtered over a million people here, in this room and others like it. Over one million people.

However, there was no smell of death.

No sounds of death.

No sight of death.

There was nothing. Nothing but concrete.

Yet...

Tess shivered, colder than she should be, as though everything – everything – in the room had died, even the very air, leaving nothing but an icy void which sucked the living warmth out of anyone foolish enough to enter.

Like the room, Tess had known death. A lot of death. So much it would have broken most people. As it almost had her. Over a five-month period in Shanghai, she'd killed fifty-three people.

Fifty-three lives. Gone.

The first six had been in self-defense. That made them easy to justify. Easy to live with.

But the seventh?

Sometimes, when she closed her eyes at night, she could still see that look on his face as she pinned his throat to the floor with her foot, about to push down. Horror mixed with resignation. Maybe even a flicker of relief. It was as if, even though he'd fought to go on living, he knew he deserved what was about to happen and had been waiting for it.

Afterward, she'd stood over him looking down. Trembling. Crying. Lost. For how long, she didn't know, but a voice in the back of her mind screamed, 'What have you done? What have you done? What the fuck have you done?'

She didn't eat or sleep for three days after that night. Despite having verified everything she'd been told about him as being true, questions had haunted her like a migraine she couldn't shake, torturing her every waking moment. Had he truly deserved to die? Had she had the right to judge? To sentence? To kill?

Tess ran her hand over the concrete wall. It was cold and smooth. Like a corpse after all the muscles had relaxed. Cracks ran through the concrete and mottled stains clung to it as if desperate not to fall to the floor and be swept away like garbage.

Fortunately for her sanity, killing had become easier. It had had to – she knew it was the only way she'd be able to make it through what she had to do back home.

So, week after week, she'd sought out targets. They'd all deserved it – she'd made damn sure of that – so she felt no shame, no guilt, no regret.

Consciously.

Subconsciously?

Hell, the dark corners of the human mind could create nightmares for even the purest of hearts.

And then came that night with Su Lin.

Everything changed that night.

Everything.

Tess strode out of the gas chamber and back outside, where she squinted at the bright sunshine flooding the crystal blue sky. Warmth once more caressed her, yet she again shivered. It was as if her subconscious wanted to shake off the horrors it had just experienced the same way a dog shakes off water.

At the entrance, she passed a tour group waiting to go into the chamber, their group leader explaining in Japanese over wireless headsets what they were about to see.

Turning left and then right, Tess cut between the two barbed wire perimeter fences and back into the primary part of the complex. There, she ambled along the main tree-lined avenue into the heart of Auschwitz.

On either side of the avenue stood two-story red brick buildings in which the prisoners had been housed. These had been a shock – she'd expected wooden shacks like she'd seen in old prisoner-of-war movies. But the luxuriousness of these buildings' construction belied their purpose. It was in one of these buildings that the genocide had started, where the Nazis had first tested the pesticide Zyklon B to see if it killed people as easily as it killed bugs.

Yes, the killing had all started here.

Just as it had all started for her in Shanghai.

That was where it had almost ended too.

It was Cheng Chao-An who'd saved her. He'd taught her not just how to go on functioning in society, but how to see what she had to do and know exactly how to do it – all without tormenting herself with questions for which there could be no satisfactory answer to a 'civilized' mind. If not for her time in the mountains, her thoughts would have haunted her, paralyzed her, brought her crashing to her knees mentally, if not physically.

Nowadays, she did what she did because it needed doing. Simple as that. In the same way a firefighter couldn't help but run into a burning building to save a child, so she couldn't turn a blind eye to some vile piece of scum abusing another innocent victim.

Fifty-three.

To the majority of the population she'd be a serial killer. To the handful who knew the truth, an angel.

Life? Life was sacrifice. And she sacrificed so that others didn't have to.

Tess sat on the strip of lawn between two of the brick buildings and then gazed around.

From the building opposite, a man with both arms plastered with tattoos shuffled out. He stopped, leaned against the wall and mopped tears from his eyes.

Tess had been in that building already so she'd seen what was inside. She didn't want to see it again. Not even in her mind's eye. But she couldn't stop the image blasting into view. In that building earlier, words, even thoughts, had failed her. Staring openmouthed, she'd stood before a room containing a mountain of human hair that the Nazis had shaved off the dead to stuff mattresses or weave into cloth for soldiers' uniforms.

With a frown, Tess heaved a breath. Even though she'd seen it for herself, she still couldn't get her head around the horrors of this place. It was simply too difficult for a person in today's world to comprehend what had gone on here.

Cross-legged on the grass, she peered up the tree-lined avenue. Auschwitz was a place of true nightmares and yet, if she hadn't known its history, it looked like a run-down college campus. Strange. Except...

It was so eerily quiet.

She checked the sky and then the trees dotted along the avenue.

Why didn't the birds sing here?

Did the authorities poison them to imbue the place with an otherworldly atmosphere befitting its hellish past? Or could animals truly sense the evils that had been done here?

An old lady hobbled toward Tess and then stood just a few feet away, studying the buildings.

After a few moments, she said in excellent English with an Eastern European accent, "Do you know where the gas chambers are, please?"

Tess pointed back the way she'd just walked. "To the end, through the wire fences, and turn left."

"Oh, it sounds quite far."

"A few minutes' walk, maybe."

"Oh, dear." The old lady heaved a breath. "Would you mind if I sit to rest a moment to get my strength back?"

For a second, Tess scrutinized her. The old lady seemed polite enough, civil enough, harmless enough, and yet, something didn't feel quite right.

Tess sighed and then gestured to the grass. "Please." She'd rather stare down a gunman than indulge in pointless chitchat, but if a person couldn't show a little tolerance and kindness here of all places, they had no soul.

"Thank you."

The old lady tottered closer and then simply stood, scanning the grass at her feet as if a chair might magically appear.

Tess held out her hand. "Can you manage?"

The lady took it and then carefully lowered herself to sit. "Thank you. I'm afraid I'm not quite as fit as I used to be."

Tess smiled politely, hoping the old lady would do her resting in silence. She did. For about three seconds.

Chapter 07

"**HAVE YOU COME** far to visit here?" said the lady.

"Not really. I was kind of passing through already."

The lady nodded, looking at Tess as if wanting to say something else, but didn't know how to start.

"Have you?" Tess said. "Do you live here?"

"No. I'm from Romania. But I had family imprisoned here, so wanted to see the place for myself while I still could."

"Your family was held here?" asked Tess. The place was horrific, but she could still remain detached because the horrors happened so long ago to people she'd never known. Suddenly having a human face put on things caused a shiver to run down her spine.

"My mother's family, yes. Her parents managed to have her smuggled out of the country. She never saw them again. It was nothing unusual back then, but it's hard to imagine now."

"You can say that again."

Now both on the same level, Tess could see the lady wasn't actually that old. Probably midfifties.

However, her sunken cheeks, gray skin, and bony arms and hands made her look decrepit.

"So where else have you passed through," said the lady, "if you don't mind me asking?"

Tess blew out a breath. "Er, Japan, China, India, Thailand. I've been around."

"My. And do you speak all those languages?"

"Enough to get by."

A wry smile crossed the lady's face. "But I bet no Romanian."

"Not a word. Sorry." A ripple of embarrassment washed over Tess. It did whenever she met a person who'd dedicated years to mastering her language while she couldn't even say something as simple as 'Hello' in theirs.

"That's okay," said the lady, her eyes sparkling with kindness. "Why would anyone learn the language of a poor country that no one cares about?"

The lady didn't seem to be having a dig, merely stating a fact. And she was right – like most people, Tess would struggle to even point to Romania on a map, so why would she bother to learn its language?

"So," said the lady, "is this a long vacation you're taking?"

"Er…" The question stumped Tess. And not for the first time – she had asked it of herself more and more lately. Why was she still in Europe instead of back in New York City following the plan she'd set in motion nearly a decade ago? How much more prepared could she be?

She'd kept telling herself she hadn't gone back yet because she wanted to see the world and experience its cultures to develop her mind as a thinking machine as much as she'd developed her body as a killing machine. More and more often though, that just seemed like an excuse.

What was holding her back?

Fear of failure?

Or fear of success? Killing had become her life in Shanghai, and that had nearly ended her – what if it became her life again back home?

But how much longer could she delay?

Every day now, a dull pain clawed inside her chest. Like homesickness on steroids. Something was trying to drag her back to the US. Something primal. Something that was becoming harder and harder to resist.

Tess didn't answer the question.

The lady locked Tess's gaze, the kindness in her eyes replaced by a burning defiance. "I saw you last night."

The words hit Tess like a shotgun blast to the chest.

Tess thought she'd misheard. "Excuse me?"

"In the park… Fighting those hooligans."

Tess remained silent. Where was she going with this? Was she going to ask for money to keep quiet?

But this revelation did explain why Tess had felt uneasy after the fight – someone had been watching her from the shadows after all. She studied the lady, trying to guess where this was heading.

"You didn't have to help that young couple," said the lady.

"Who else was going to help them?"

"The police."

Tess was sure the lady hadn't meant to be funny, but she couldn't help but snicker. "Yeah, right."

"You don't have much faith in the authorities?"

Tess shot her a sideways glance.

"Aren't they there to help you?"

"At best, they're there as a deterrent, at worst, as a clean-up crew."

The lady thought for a moment. "But why risk your own safety? You could just have walked away."

No, she couldn't. Not when she had the skills she had. It would be like a doctor walking away from the scene of an accident leaving someone to bleed out on the street.

The woman's frail, gray hand reached over. She placed a photograph of a woman in Tess's lap. The woman was around Tess's age, had a striking, angular face and long, flowing brown hair. The woman's hair reminded Tess of how hers used to be, before she'd hacked it all off to barely shoulder length that night in Shanghai. That night that had started everything.

"I'm Elena Petrescu," said the lady. "This is Catalina, my daughter. She's been missing since yesterday morning."

"Missing?"

"I—" Elena's chin quivered. She hung her head for a moment, and then tried again. "I can't find her anywhere."

"I hope you don't mind if I'm blunt, but how do you know she isn't just shacked up with some guy she met in a bar?"

"As I said, this is something of a pilgrimage, not a beer-fueled vacation."

Tess nodded. That was a fair reason for discounting a drunken one-night stand. "Has anyone asked you for money?"

"No."

"So what have the police said?"

"I don't want a clean-up crew," Elena said. "I want a detective."

Tess winced. "Sorry, but you're talking to the wrong person – I can look after myself, yes, but I'm no detective."

Elena took a roll of banknotes out of her pocket. "I can pay."

From the roll's size, it looked a substantial amount, but the first was only a ten-zloty note, suggesting they all were. If there was even a couple of hundred dollars, Tess would be amazed.

"It's not about money," Tess said. "I just don't think I can help you."

The woman placed her hand on Tess's. The outlines of the bones and many of the veins stood out as clearly as if Tess had X-ray vision.

"I understand." Her chin quivering again, Elena hung her head.

"I'm sorry."

Elena nodded. After a moment, she looked up.

"As you can see," Elena said, her voice wavering, "I'm not in the best of health." She patted Tess's hand. "All I wanted was to see my Catalina one last time and to tell her I love her. I'm all she has."

A lump in Tess's throat choked her words. For a moment, she was back in that hospital room, back beside that bed, back holding someone for the last time. Except she hadn't known it was for the last time. That heartache had lived with her for years. Could she deny this mother one last chance to hold her daughter and say goodbye?

Chapter 08

ELENA HANDED THE rotund waitress thirty zlotys and said something in Polish. The woman laughed and then toddled away, zigzagging through the bar's scattered rectangular tables.

With only local clientele, the backstreet bar near Elena's hostel was a big square room with none of the quaintness of the tourist bar Tess had visited the previous night. Its only decoration stretched to photographs hung on the walls of what Tess guessed were Polish celebrities, but she didn't recognize a single one of them.

Elena held out her beer for a toast. Tess had paid for their meal and had wanted to pay for the beer too, but Elena was simply too proud to accept endless charity, so she had insisted on buying. "To finding Cat."

Lifting her drink, Tess toasted Elena. "To finding Catalina. Na zdrovie." Even though she didn't intend on staying in Poland long, Tess had picked up a few of the more useful phrases such as hello, please, thank you, ATM, toilet, and cheers.

Elena playfully wagged a finger at her. "In Romanian, we say 'noroc'."

Tess chinked glasses with her again. "Noroc."

"To finding Cat and to your first Romanian word."

Over the rim of her glass, Tess surveyed her fellow drinkers. She'd give anyone one hundred to one against seeing any of the three men she'd beaten to a pulp last night, but that pudgy fourth guy had run away. She didn't want to be clobbered from behind and kicked senseless while she was down, so she had even more reason than usual to remain constantly aware of her environment.

Putting her glass on the table, Tess couldn't help but chuckle to herself – the frail old lady who'd approached her in Auschwitz was now chugging away on her beer like a teenage boy at his first frat party.

Half of her drink gone in one go, Elena placed her glass on the table with a satisfying ahhh. She wiped a little froth from her top lip.

"Thirsty?" Tess said.

"Because of my medication, I haven't been able to enjoy a drink for months."

"So you've stopped your medication?"

"No, I've stopped caring. For now at least."

"But won't alcohol interfere with your meds?"

Elena rolled her eyes. "Don't you start. I get enough of that from Cat." As if to make a point, she took another gulp of beer.

Exhaling with another ahhh, Elena cradled her glass and gazed longingly at the golden liquid. "Oh, that's good. Not as good as our beer, but..." She looked up. "I think you say 'it hit the spot', yes?"

Tess snickered. "Yeah, we do." The woman's grasp of English was excellent. In fact, it was better than a considerable number of born-and-bred New Yorkers Tess could name.

As Elena put her glass down, she looked Tess square in the eye. "Would you mind if I asked you a question?"

Tess shrugged as she took a sip.

"Why did you help those people last night?"

Again Tess shrugged, as if what she'd done was nothing that anyone wouldn't have done in those circumstances. "Right place, right time."

Elena squinted at Tess, obviously mulling over that answer. After a moment, she said, "No, it was... hmm... I don't know the word. Er, you looked like you knew what was going to happen and were waiting for it, not like a, er, a by-passer."

Tess cringed at the thought of where the conversation looked to be heading. "A passer-by."

"That's it – passer-by. Thank you. So, you knew, didn't you? You weren't a passer-by, but knew there was going to be trouble and that you could handle it. How? Have you been in the military? Police?" Elena looked at her, eyebrows raised with expectation.

Tess shook her head. "No, nothing like that."

The woman across the table was a complete stranger. At this point, Tess couldn't risk giving away any information that wasn't strictly necessary to getting the job done and finding the missing woman. That said, any fool seeing her in action could tell she was highly-trained, so there was nothing to be gained from denying it. It would be best to throw the woman a bone and let her gnaw on it.

To tell a convincing lie, Tess had developed three basic principles: her 'just enough' rules. Rule #1: give just enough information that it sounded plausible. Rule #2: use just enough subject-specific jargon that it sounded real. Rule #3: reveal just enough detail that it left options for follow-up lies.

Tess said, "A few years back, I had a boyfriend who taught Shotokan karate at the local Y, so I got him to teach me some of his best moves. It comes in handy every so often, but at the time, it was just for fun."

"Just for fun?"

"Uh-huh." Tess smiled as sincerely as she could, then took another sip of beer while gazing around the bar, as if her glass was something behind which she could hide.

Unfortunately, 'just enough' just wasn't enough for some people.

"When I was your age, I took a six-month judo course." The tiniest of wistful smiles flickered across her face as she obviously thought back to a time when she was young and probably more importantly, fit. "Boy, I loved throwing the big guys around the dojo as if they were rag dolls. Such fantastic fun." She sighed. "But on a trip to Bucharest, I got mugged by a guy barely taller than I am, so I figured I'd use my judo on him and teach him a damn good lesson. I got a bloody nose and a broken arm for trying that."

The woman wasn't going to let this go. "I guess I just got lucky." Tess tipped her glass toward Elena. "It really is damn good beer, isn't it?"

"I think you're being a little modest putting what you did down to luck. But that's not what I meant to ask. Sorry, my English isn't great."

"Believe me, your English is excellent. How come you speak it so well?" By asking a question that didn't allow a simple one word answer, Tess directed the conversation away from her past.

"My husband. No, what I meant to say is, you weren't a passer-by, but purposefully went there to protect those people. Like a... what do you call it... a guardian angel."

For a third time, Tess shrugged. Her attempt to change the subject from her combat skills to Elena's language skills had failed dismally, so maybe if she just said nothing, Elena would either get the message, or move on to another subject simply to end the awkward pause in the conversation.

There was quiet for a couple of seconds.

"So why?" asked Elena. "What happened to you that makes you want to protect people like that?"

Pictures flooded Tess's mind. Pictures of blood. So much blood. So much, it was as if someone had thrown a bucketful over her. The memory was still so crystal clear. Even after all these years. Like the image had been cauterized onto her brain.

She stared down at the table and the drink she was grasping in her right hand. A tiny rivulet of water ran down through the condensation enveloping the glass. Tess focused on the droplet. Focused on the light dancing in that tiny sparkling orb. Trying to center herself. Calm herself. Forget.

But underneath the table, her left hand balled into a fist so tight that her fingernails dug into her palm.

Then she heard it. As clearly as if it was coming from right beside her that very moment. That sound she dreaded. That sound which haunted so many of her dreams – a gurgling, rasping breathing.

An empty ache in her gut started sucking all the life out of her, as if her stomach had been torn open and was slowly being prized wider and wider apart.

Despite all the time that had passed, all the horrific things she'd seen and... all the horrific things she'd done, she could still feel that blood on her hands. Wet. Warm. Oozing. She'd tried to apply pressure just like she'd been taught. Tried to stop it. But there was just so much. So, so much.

Maybe if she'd tried harder. Tried longer. Maybe... Maybe she could have saved–

Elena gently grasped Tess's hand, jolting Tess out of her waking nightmare, and said, "Oh, me and my big mouth, hey? Here you are helping me out of the goodness of your heart and I'm interrogating you like some sadistic SS officer. I'm sorry, Tess. I didn't mean to upset you."

Tess wondered what element of her body language had given away her agony for it to be so obvious. Maybe her eye had twitched, or the blood had drained from her face, or her hand had trembled on her glass. No matter. If she'd prevented one thing from happening, her hurt would only have manifested in another. Despite all her best efforts and all her mental conditioning, some wounds, some memories just couldn't be buried deeply enough.

She winced a smile at the lady. To give herself a moment to gather her thoughts, she took a long, slow swig of her beer.

Elena smiled back, a sadness in her eyes. "It's obviously painful, so I won't ask again. I'm sorry." She shook her head. "Cat always says being nosy will be the death of me." She took another drink, too.

Tess gave a slight nod in acknowledgement. She appreciated Elena's gesture, but to be safe, she'd force the conversation in a completely different direction.

Her gaze drifted to Elena's hand that was holding the glass and to the three parallel scars which ran across the back of it. Elena had obviously been slashed by something sharp, but the scars were faded, not enflamed, and flat to the rest of the hand, not pronounced, all of which suggested it was an old injury.

Aside from being desperate to change the subject, if Tess was going to put her life on the line, she needed to know it was for the right reasons and that Elena and her daughter were truly worth fighting for. To judge that, she needed information. The scar presented an ideal opportunity to dig into this family's history through a seemingly innocuous comment.

"Talking about painful – that must have been nasty." With a flick of her gaze, Tess gestured to Elena's hand.

"Hmmm?"

"Your hand."

Elena twisted her hand around to look at it. "Oh, yes, it was. I got too close to a bear."

Tess's eyes widened with surprise. "A bear?" She had expected it to be a work injury, an assault, a car accident, anything but an animal attack. How the devil did anyone get too close to a bear unless they were a complete imbecile?

"I was trying to feed it," Elena said, as if she expected that to explain things.

So the woman truly was an imbecile. "You were trying to feed a wild bear?"

"No, a dancing bear. I volunteered at a sanctuary that rescued them."

"Ah." As a young girl, Tess had been so close to her black cat Tickle that it had followed her everywhere like a little dog. She'd been devastated when the poor little thing had died of leukemia when it was only six. She'd cried every day for a month. One day, she'd love to work with animals. One day, when this life was far behind her. One day, after she'd finally reaped her vengeance back home. Maybe then, those memories would finally stop haunting her.

"We have thousands of bears in Transylvania," said Elena, "but unfortunately, many people only see them as a way to make easy money."

"Transylvania?"

"Uh-huh."

"Transylvania where Dracula lives?"

Another wry smile crept across Elena's face. "Transylvania where Vlad Tepes lived in the fifteenth century. You probably know him as Vlad the Impaler. He was the inspiration for Dracula."

"Oh, I didn't know that."

"Anyway, we rescued bears people had trapped. Most of them traumatized from years of abuse or neglect." She caressed her scarred hand. "This was Tia. My favorite. Her owner kept her as a tourist attraction outside his restaurant, but the problem was, camera flashes frightened her, so she always moved and ruined people's photos. So her owner stuck needles in her eyes to blind her – if she couldn't see the flash, she wouldn't move, so happy tourist."

"Jesus." Tess winced at the thought of it. "He stuck needles in her eyes?"

Elena nodded. "She was almost dead when we found her. I nursed her back to health but forgot she was basically still a wild animal and got too close one day. It was my own stupid fault, not Tia's."

56

Tess studied the three scars and then her drinking partner. Elena brought light into a world overwhelmed by darkness. Should Tess help her? Like there could be any other answer to that question but one. Tess would do everything she could to find Catalina. And along the way, she'd learn more about Tia's owner. He was one real nice guy she'd love to meet.

Elena said, "So, do you have any idea how we might find Cat?"

With a red pen, Tess tapped an area she'd circled on the free tourist map of Krakow Elena had picked up in her hostel, a map exactly like the one Catalina had followed.

"We're sure this is where Cat was looking for work?" asked Tess.

"As far as I know. She looked here" – Elena pointed to another area – "the day before."

"Okay. But you couldn't find anyone in this area who'd seen her."

"No."

"What time did you try?"

"Last night, around nine thirty, when I just couldn't settle anymore without doing something. I wandered the streets for hours – that's how I spotted you."

Tess jabbed with the pen to emphasize her point. "You see, that could be the problem."

"What could?" She took another swig of her beer.

Again, Tess tapped the map with her pen. "Well… if Cat tried all these places first thing in the morning, but you went there in the late evening, it's very possible no one had seen her because the daytime staff had been replaced by the nighttime staff."

Elena stared at her. A tiny smile crept across her face.

Tess sipped her beer. "What?"

"And you thought you weren't a detective."

"Yeah, well I'll pat myself on the back when we find Cat." Tess planted her finger firmly in the center of the circled area on the map. "I want to go here tomorrow morning. See if we can speak to people who were actually working around the time we think Cat was there. Is that okay?"

"Oh, don't worry about me, Tess. Anything that needs doing. Anything. You don't even need to ask, just tell me and it's as good as done."

"Okay, so we'll meet outside Town Hall Tower at six thirty a.m. Now, about this guy." She tapped a piece of paper on which was scrawled the name Jacek Grabowski, a cell phone number, an address, and a web link.

Tess took out her smartphone. When she'd been in the Far East, she'd never wanted a cell phone. In fact, she'd hated the thought of having one all but surgically attached to her, as ninety-nine percent of the world had these days. Since she'd started making her way back home, however, having one had helped her with travel arrangements and with online research that might enable her to find who she needed to find back home.

She called the number Elena's phone had registered as being the one from which Cat had called. It rang and rang and rang. Didn't even go to voicemail.

Listening to it ring, she shook her head at Elena.

"No one ever answered when I tried it," Elena said.

Tess let it ring.

Elena coughed. Just a gentle tickle-in-the-throat kind of cough. Except it didn't go away and she coughed again. And again. And the coughing didn't stop. Her whole body shook. Elena held her hands in front of her mouth, as her head jerked back and forth.

Tess put her phone down and held Elena's beer out to her, hoping a drink would ease the cough.

Elena reached for it, but was coughing so violently, her hand hit the glass and splashed beer on the table.

Tess moved around to Elena's side of the table and held the glass up to her lips. Elena managed a couple of sips. The hacking started to subside.

The rotund waitress who'd laughed at Elena's joke appeared beside them and said something.

"I'm sorry," Tess said, "I don't speak Polish."

The waitress held out a mentholated candy, the kind people sucked to help a tickly throat.

"Oh, thank you," Tess said. "Er... Dziekuje." She placed one on the table next to Elena's beer.

The waitress nodded and disappeared.

Her coughing under control, Elena patted Tess's hand. "Thank you. I'll be okay now."

Tess retook her seat. "Do you want me to fetch your medication for you?"

Elena shot her a sideways glance. "I only take it because Cat nags me to."

"Why? Doesn't it do any good?"

Elena popped the candy in her mouth. "About as much good as this." She must have seen the sadness on Tess's face, because the lady reached over and squeezed her hand. "Please, don't waste a second worrying about me. I've had a wonderful life. All I want now is to see Cat safe again. And you're already helping me with that."

"But—"

"Please." Elena gestured to the map on the table and the notes they'd made. "Somehow, I don't think we have a lot of time."

Tess took a slow breath. No, Elena was right. If they were to find Cat, they had to start before the trail got too cold.

"Okay, so this address." Tess held up the piece of paper with the address Cat had given over the phone. "You said you'd tried to find it."

"I spoke to six taxi drivers. None of them had any idea where it was."

"And the website?"

With a shrug, Elena shook her head.

Tess typed into her phone: KrakowWellnessCenter.com.

Instead of a website appearing, all Tess got was an error message.

She tried replacing .com with .org, then .net, and then all the other top-level domains she could think of.

Nothing.

Finally, she tried .pl, the top-level domain for Poland. Again, the only thing to appear was an error message.

She googled 'Krakow Wellness Center' but instead of a definitive organization appearing in the results, pages of spas, hotels, and resorts materialized.

Elena said, "I was sure I'd written it down correctly, but maybe I didn't."

"Maybe." Tess tried to say it as upbeat as she could.

That was a possible – and the most preferable – explanation for her not being able to find the website.

However, a website was simply a collection of files, so if a person had all of them stored on an electronic device, such as a tablet or a phone, they could look at a fully functioning website without it or they ever having to be online. Anyone else using that device would have no idea they weren't looking at a real, live site.

Tess felt that tingling sensation again. The same one she'd had the previous night when she'd known someone was in the shadows watching. Her instincts said this was not a simple case of someone going missing, but that it was far more than that. Far darker than that. So dark that she didn't want to discuss it with Elena until she was certain for fear of how it would upset her. But she didn't need to.

Elena stared unblinking. "This is bad, isn't it?"

Tess didn't reply. Elena already knew the answer.

Elena hadn't received any demands for money so that left only two reasons for why someone would abduct a beautiful woman – rape or murder. If not both.

Bad? Bad wasn't the word for it. There was no way the situation could get any worse. Unless…

No, Tess couldn't think like that. They needed to stay positive. Maybe she could yet offer Elena some reassurance.

"Look at it this way, there's been no local news story about the police finding a body. That's a big positive. Very big. That's what we have to focus on."

"Okay," Elena said, forcing a brave smile which was belied by the sadness in her eyes.

Cat might be trapped in a living nightmare, but at least it was still 'living'. Hopefully. If only Tess could reach her in time. But could she?

Chapter 09

TESS STOOD OUTSIDE Elena's hostel. In the entrance, a black plastic bag of trash had burst, spilling out water bottles, used toiletries and fast-food packaging. The place looked as inviting as a brothel that offered free crab cream at the door.

Tess waved as Elena entered. "See you in the morning."

As she turned away, a gang of six young men strutted down the street heading toward the bars in the Old Town. In what appeared to be some kind of English, they talked about a 'bird' in the last bar who had 'norks as big as Tony's head'. From the context, Tess guessed 'bird' meant woman and 'norks' were breasts.

In the middle of the group, a guy in a white soccer jersey emblazoned with the word 'England' shouted at Tess. His slang and odd accent made what he said almost incomprehensible.

"Alright, love. Now your mam's away to her pit, how about a pint with me and our kid? This is his stag do but he's still a free man till a fortnight Saturday."

Away to her pit? Fortnight Saturday? Stag do? What the hell part of England were they from?

She smiled to placate him, but said, "That's okay, thanks."

His friend with a huge pimple on the side of his nose said, "Leave it, Gazza. I tell you, you won't believe the vag you can get here for a hundred zlotys."

Gazza shoved his friend on the shoulder. "I'm not sodding paying for it."

"A hundred zlotys? That's only twenty quid, you tosser."

"Twenty quid? So why didn't you say so?"

Pimple Nose grinned. "Jesus, you're going to cream your pants in Red Riot. Cream, I tell you."

They passed by.

Having seen Elena safely home, Tess zigzagged through backstreets toward her own hotel, deep in thought about what might have happened to Catalina and what might be the best approach to finding her. As she crossed a junction, at the far end of the street on her left, neon signs lured customers into bars.

She stopped.

Scrutinized the signs and silhouettes of people milling about.

A bar might not be such a bad idea.

She marched down toward the nightlife.

As far as she knew, prostitution was legal in Poland but brothels weren't – in theory. Because of the tourist dollar, Krakow's authorities chose to turn a blind eye. Maybe the Brits' idea of looking for a cheap lay had opened up possibilities she hadn't considered and could give her a head start in the search for Cat.

Tess spotted the club the Brits had mentioned: Red Riot. The building's medieval architecture was a stark contrast to the pulsing strobe lights shafting through its arched windows.

A guy with a barrel of a chest guarded the door. He smiled as he let her enter. Inside, the lower two floors had been knocked out and lights suspended on a metal rig hung from the double-height ceiling. They spun and flashed and swept in arcs, their light reflecting off the walls and floor, which had been decorated in a silver metallic effect.

Tess wriggled through the revelers to the bar and ordered a bottle of local beer. It cost twice what she'd paid in the bar with Elena, but then, that bar hadn't offered a light show or opportunities for cheap sex.

Taking a swig of her beer, she surveyed the scene for who might help her with her questions, while music thumped up through the floor and into her feet.

She hoped her logic was sound. Prostitution was legal here, so johns didn't suffer the degree of social stigma they did in the States. There was a fair chance that a person who would abduct a woman might also regularly pay for sex. If he did, the hookers he used would likely know more than just his name.

On the other hand, if he didn't use prostitutes but was a known sicko, word would have spread through the hooking community that women had to be wary of him.

Either way, the local working girls might have information which could be helpful.

Of course, he might not use prostitutes and might appear a decent, upstanding member of the community, which would make this a total waste of time. But an investigation had to start somewhere. And right now, this was as good a place as any.

A red-haired girl bursting out of a skimpy black dress lounged on a stool alone at the bar. She did not have a drink in front of her. While the occasional local woman might venture in here alone, or even the odd lone female tourist, Tess doubted they'd be allowed to sit at the bar very long without a drink.

Tess meandered over and stood beside the girl. "Hi."

Red Head raised an eyebrow and panned her gaze over Tess. "Hi."

"Do you speak English?"

"Why?" she said with a Polish accent. "Are you looking for a good time?"

Tess winked. "Oh, I'm always looking for a good time."

A girl with a jet-black bob moseyed over and slung her arm around Red Head's shoulders. She smiled at Tess. "Are we having a party?"

"Maybe," said Tess, "but maybe you can help me – I'm looking for my friend Jacek Grabowski. Do you know him?"

"Why don't you buy us a drink so we can get comfortable and talk," Red Head said.

A drink, even at twice the normal cost, was a cheap price for information. Tess waved to one of the bartenders, who looked at who she was with and then nodded without even asking what she wanted to order.

"So do you know Jacek Grabowski?"

"No," said Red Head.

Tess looked at the other woman who just shook her head.

65

Great. Just a couple of freeloaders. Hell, how did guys put up with this crap when they tried picking up women?

The bartender brought each of the women a brown colored drink in a glass about twice the size of a shot glass.

He held out his hand to Tess. "Two hundred zloty."

Tess thought he said two hundred zlotys, but that couldn't be right. "Excuse me?"

Holding up two fingers, he said again, "Two hundred zloty."

"No, no, no." Tess pointed to the two women. "I only ordered drinks for these two."

The bartender stared her coldly in the eye. "Two drinks – two hundred zloty."

That was fifty bucks. No way was she getting scammed into paying fifty bucks for what was probably worth about fifty cents.

"Come on," Tess said, "those aren't a hundred zloty each."

The bartender waved to someone behind Tess.

A big guy with stubble and a squint reared over her. "Problem?"

"Yeah" – Tess pointed at the bartender – "this guy is trying to rip me off for two hundred zloty for two drinks."

Squint nodded. "Two hundred zloty is price."

"Not for me it ain't."

She turned to leave, but Squint grabbed her arm. His fingers clawed into her bicep.

She glared up into his face. "You're hurting me."

"Two hundred zloty or it hurt more."

Chapter 10

TESS GLANCED AT the girls at the bar as the brutal truth clicked: they weren't hookers, not even freeloaders. No, they were employed by the bar solely to scam gullible people into buying them extortionately priced drinks. If the customer refused to pay, heavies moved in. No way would an average joe get out of here without paying or bleeding.

She cowered behind her hands. "Okay. I'll pay. Please, don't hurt me."

Squint relaxed his grip, obviously assuming his work was done.

"I need to get my money." She gestured to her black backpack.

He nodded.

Crouching on the floor, Tess unslung her backpack, opened it and rooted inside on the pretext of looking for her money. There was at least one other bouncer in here who she'd passed when she'd come in, but she'd no idea how many others were around.

Squint ignored her and shared a joke in Polish with the two women who'd gotten her into this mess.

Those few seconds were all Tess needed. She slipped on her black leather gloves and balled her fists. Inside her gloves, the strip of eighth-of-an-inch-thick steel curved over her knuckles to hug them perfectly.

As she stood up, Squint turned back to her and pointed to the bartender. "You pay now."

Smiling as coyly as she could, Tess picked up one of the drinks. "Look, no hard feelings, huh?"

She held it out to him. Let him think he'd won. Let him think he was the big man. Let him think a skinny woman could never be any kind of threat.

With more of a sneer than a smile, he reached for the drink.

Tess threw it in his face.

He automatically pulled his hands up to his eyes.

Tess stamped through his knee. The bone crunched so loudly she heard it over the thumping music.

He cried out and staggered to one side as all around, people scattered, not wanting to be dragged into violence.

Tess slammed a right hook into the side of Squint's head and then hammered a kick into his other leg.

Squint crashed into the silver floor. With a broken knee, he wouldn't be standing unaided for months, so she could rule him out as any further threat.

Something pounded Tess square in the back.

She crashed forward to sprawl over the bar. Bottles skidded away and smashed on the floor.

From the force of the blow, the angle of delivery, and the size of the impact area, her training told her someone had kicked her. She'd be bruised tomorrow, but adrenaline deadened her to the immediate pain.

A follow-up attack would likely come from her right because most people were right-handed. Instinctively, instead of turning to face her attacker, she ducked and spun away to her left.

That instant, another kick sliced across the top of the bar from her right, smashing through drinks people had left to stand.

Glass shards showered Tess.

She cowered for the briefest of moments, then, fists up, Tess faced her attacker.

A tall skinny bouncer stormed at her. He'd obviously studied martial arts, probably Tae Kwon Do from his form. He launched a sweeping roundhouse kick at her head. The kick was so graceful, it must have looked amazing to the bystanders stood at a safe distance.

Tess stepped in closer to him. To those watching, moving closer to danger must have looked suicidal, but they hadn't spent seven years in the Far East learning how to kill with their bare hands.

While the bouncer's leg was arcing toward her through the air, Tess's elbow thundered into his knee.

No sooner had her blow landed, than she flung backfist with the same hand into his face. His nose exploded, blood spurting out across his cheeks.

Grabbing him around the back of the neck, she hauled him forward and slammed her knee into his gut.

Fearing someone might clobber her from behind again, Tess glanced around while her still holding her opponent.

A fat bouncer with a ponytail pushed his way through the mesmerized crowd.

Twisting around, Tess threw the tall bouncer over her hip so he crashed to the floor in the direct line of the fat bouncer.

This fat bouncer proved more agile than he looked and jumped over his colleague.

Tess sidestepped and hammered a kick at him as he sailed through the air, kicking his legs from under him.

The fat bouncer crashed forward but managed to throw his hands up to protect himself as he smashed into the bar.

Tess stomped on his ankle to put him out of action too. He reared back, face contorted in pain.

Tess spun around. Faced the crowd. Fists up ready to strike.

The bouncer who'd been on the door and let her in was standing on the edge of the crowd. He looked at his three battered colleagues at Tess's feet, then held his hands up and backed away.

Like the story of Moses and the Red Sea, the crowd parted, making a clear route to the door for Tess.

Keeping her fists up, gaze panning around for a threat, she headed out.

As she passed, the Brit with a pimple on his nose nudged Gazza. "Fuck me, Gazza! And you thought you were going to shag that? Jesus, she'd have bloody killed you, mate."

Tess exited the club.

She shook her head. Jesus, why was it so difficult to have a quiet goddamn drink in this country?

She marched along the street, regularly checking behind her to ensure the bouncers hadn't decided there was strength in even greater numbers.

Now what? Another bar or call it quits for the day?

Chapter 11

WITH A STUNNING blue sky declaring what a beautiful world it was, Tess strolled across the cobbled square toward Town Hall Tower. In an area that could hold thousands of people, only the odd business person prepared for another day's toil. The emptiness gave the square a strange feel. Like in a horror movie after a plague had decimated the population and the camera panned over deserted city streets which normally teemed with people.

Passing the Cloth Hall, its colonnade of stone arches more a setting for a romance than a horror movie, Tess checked her watch – 6:26 a.m. She'd give anyone ten-to-one odds she wouldn't see Elena for at least another hour. Maybe two. After Elena had insisted on another couple of beers in the bar last night, Tess wouldn't be surprised if she didn't show up at all. To Tess, three strong European beers was a decent drink, but to fragile old Elena, with barely an ounce of meat on her bones, it must have been like a falling into a vat of whisky and trying to drink her way out.

Tess rounded the corner of the tower. She needn't have worried – Elena waved at her, sitting on the steps between the two stone lions.

Well, if Cat had the strength her mother had, they had a good chance of finding her before it was too late. Unless, of course, it was already too late.

"Morning," Tess said with a grin, "I was worried you wouldn't make it on time."

Elena looked bemused. "Why?"

"Because of all the beer last night."

"Three beers?" Elena laughed. "Oh my, you should have seen me when I was your age."

"You enjoyed partying?"

"No. I just enjoyed an average social life. We Eastern Europeans enjoy our beer – why do you think we have so many of them? So, where are we going first?"

Tess took a breath, not wanting to ruin the atmosphere. "You do appreciate that what we find could be very upsetting."

Elena's lightheartedness vanished in an instant. "More upsetting than the pictures I see in my mind every time I think about the nightmare Cat's trapped in?"

"Let's hope not," Tess said, "Okay, before the streets are overrun by tourists, I want to walk the route we think Cat took to see if we can find anything she might have dropped."

After the fight the previous night, Tess had gone to bed. Red Riot's staff would have circulated warnings about her to other bars, so there had been little point in visiting anywhere else. Now, all she could do was go back to the original plan she'd formulated before she'd heard the Brits chatting.

Elena held out her hand to Tess. Tess took it and eased the lady up off the steps. Elena groaned as she clambered to her feet.

"I'm sorry," said Elena, "but it takes me a while to get going once I stop. So where first?"

Tess pointed to Bracka Street in the area of the Old Town they'd identified last night as where Cat had probably been looking for work just before she disappeared.

Walking slowly, Tess said, "Do you remember exactly what Cat was wearing and had with her?"

"Yes, it was what she'd had to wear for two days because all our clothes had been stolen with everything else."

"So did she have pants or a dress, a bag, an umbrella, a head scarf...?"

Without any hesitation, Elena said, "White canvas shoes, pale blue skirt, white blouse, navy canvas purse. No scarf. No umbrella."

"And you'd recognize any of those if you saw them?"

"I think so, yes."

"Did she have sunglasses with her? Jewelry? A handkerchief? Anything distinctive in her purse?"

Elena thought for a moment. "She wore a thin silver necklace and matching anklet, and silver ear studs. And she had her passport and some personal documents with her; a little money; a small wallet with photos she always carried with her and, er... er... I don't know what it's called – a small green plant with leaves – it usually has three but sometimes you find one with four so you keep it for good luck."

"A four-leaf clover?"

"Yes, she always kept it with her in a little plastic wallet."

"Okay. So if she was, er…" How could she put it without Elena picturing horrors?

"If she was taken?" Elena said.

Tess nodded solemnly. "She could easily have lost some jewelry or something from her purse." She pointed to Bracka. "We'll walk up one side and down the other to make sure we don't miss anything."

If they found something, maybe it would be strong enough evidence for the police to take the possibility of an abduction seriously. Tess had little faith in the police – they'd failed her so badly, how could she ever trust them again? – but the more eyes that were looking for Cat the better.

But whether the police became involved or not, finding something that belonged to Cat would show them where she'd been taken. Finding the scene of the crime would be the first step in solving it.

Shuffling along the sidewalk, Tess inspected the cracks between the uneven paving stones and the trash in the gutter, hoping they'd find something, but praying it wouldn't be bloodstained.

They scoured the left-hand side of the street further than they'd decided Cat might have ventured – going beyond the Franciscan Church, famous for its Art Nouveau interior which blazed with murals in blues, greens and yellows, and on into the far side of the park which circled the Old Town. Afterward, they crawled down the other side of the street, even taking a detour up a side alley that might have caught Cat's eye.

Despite proceeding at a torturously slow pace to ensure they searched every inch of both sidewalks and the road, they found nothing.

They plodded back to the square and up the next street leading off it.

To their dismay, the same search methodology delivered the same sluggish results – absolutely squat.

Unfortunately, Krakow was now waking up and going about its day – traffic grunted along its narrow streets and pedestrians bustled along the sidewalks.

Elena stopped and leaned over the edge of the curb to peer between the bars of a grate in the gutter.

Having to move out of the way of a woman with a baby stroller, Tess looked up from examining every tiny crevice in the sidewalk. "Elena, I— Oh, Jesus!"

Tess lunged at the lady. She grabbed her by the shoulder and yanked her back from the curb. A delivery truck tore by that could have taken her head off.

Searching the sidewalk with pedestrians rushing all around had become more and more frustrating, while searching the road had become more and more hair-raising. No, it was time for a different tack, for a more hands-on approach.

"It's getting too busy." Tess looked at her watch: 8:10. "I think it's time we try to trace the places Cat went to and see where that takes us."

"If you think that's best."

They tramped back to the first street they'd searched. Most cafés and hotels were open, so Cat would have been actively looking for work at this time yesterday. If they could find the right place and the right staff, they could map out where she'd been and when. If they could discover the last place and time Cat was

75

spotted, maybe they could find a witness to what had become of her or, better yet, CCTV footage from a security camera.

Tess pulled open the big wooden door of Hotel Amber Wawel.

"Remember, just as we discussed – don't get emotional, don't get confrontational, treat it as a simple inquiry, like asking for directions. Ask if they were working around this time yesterday, ask if they remember Cat, and if not, ask if anyone else was working who you could talk to. Oh, and ask if they know Jacek Grabowski."

Tess couldn't speak Polish, so unless the staff they encountered spoke English, Elena was going to have to do all the talking. Plus, on her travels, Tess had found that talking to someone in their own language often made them more amenable and more likely to help her. She prayed that tactic would pay off now because so far, they had squat.

Chapter 12

WITH AN ASSORTMENT of large, leafy plants in bronze pots dotted about, the hotel looked pleasant enough, though the dust and cobwebs on the plants didn't bode well for the cleanliness of the rooms.

Tess and Elena approached Reception. A man wearing round-rim glasses smiled and said something with a light, welcoming tone.

Elena said hello and asked him a question, to which he nodded. Then she showed him her photo of Cat.

He looked at it, but then winced and said something in a deeper tone of voice. Tess didn't need Elena to translate.

Back on the street, Tess squeezed Elena's arm. "Don't get disheartened. That was only the first place. I'm not going to stop until we find out what's happened. Okay?"

Elena patted Tess's hand, but said nothing. Had Elena realized how carefully she'd chosen her words? Tess hadn't said she wouldn't stop until she found Cat, but until she found what had happened. There was a gigantic difference. But she couldn't promise what she knew she couldn't deliver.

Methodically, they moved along the street, going to every hotel, hostel, café, and restaurant at which they imagined Cat might have sought work. No one had seen Cat.

If the basic premise of their plan was flawed – if they'd identified the wrong part of the Old Town in which to search – their job would be ten times more difficult because they'd have to scour the entire city. And that created a huge problem: time.

Tess heaved a breath, staring at her watch but not actually registering the time. She had to pick up Cat's trail now. Not that afternoon, not tomorrow, not the next day. Now. If she didn't, it would become harder and harder to find her because witnesses' memories would fail and physical evidence would either degrade or be lost completely.

But so far, they'd found no evidence and no witnesses. That meant some element of their plan was wrong.

Trudging back to the square, Tess unzipped her leather jacket, the day turning out to be not just bright, but warm.

"Are you sure it was this area Cat was going to explore?"

"This is where she said, yes," Elena said.

"So maybe it's the kind of work we've got wrong so we're going to the wrong kinds of places. What other kind of work could she have looked for, other than cleaning rooms or washing dishes?"

Elena took a gulp from the bottle of water Tess had bought her and then said, "She can't speak Polish to be able to talk to people, so she couldn't be a store clerk, a waitress, or anything like that. What other kind of work could she do?"

Elena's logic was sound, so if their plan was flawed, it was in the area they were searching.

But that caused its own headache.

They had no option, but to continue until they'd exhausted all the possibilities in this part of the Old Town. They couldn't risk giving up because the very next place which they skipped could be the very place they'd stumble upon Cat's trail.

Back in the square, street performers and buskers attracted small crowds. Appreciative audience members dropped cash into hats, bags or instrument cases.

As they ambled along the gray cobbles, Tess paused for a moment to watch a man in a blue-and-white striped tuxedo juggling two carving knives, an axe and a meat cleaver. Sergei had taught her how to throw a blade, but she'd never dreamed of juggling with them. She dropped five zlotys into a brown Burlap bag in front of him and turned away. Elena had disappeared.

Tess slowly turned in a circle, studying all the faces of the people enjoying the sun in this beautiful medieval city. She spotted Elena talking to a man with a braided beard sitting at an easel. Dotted around on the patch of square he'd claimed were pencil drawings of celebrities. They were so good that anyone could see at a glance who they were supposed to be – Marilyn Monroe, James Dean, Bruce Lee, Elvis.

Tess waited for two brown horses to plod past pulling a white, four-wheel carriage, the family riding inside grinning from ear to ear as their young son took selfies of them all squashed together on the rear seat.

Before Tess could cross, a couple of guys on rented Segways zipped by. Finally, she ambled over to Elena.

The bearded artist studied the photo of Cat and nodded, then handed it back and said something in Polish. Elena thanked him.

"Has he seen her?" asked Tess.

"I wasn't asking about that. I wanted to know if he could copy my photograph but make it much bigger."

Tess took Elena's hands in hers. "Listen, I can imagine what's going through your mind right now, but you have to stay positive. Unless we learn something to the contrary, Cat is alive. And as long as she's alive, we can find her. Okay?"

A tear trickled down Elena's cheek. She squeezed Tess's hands. "Thank you. I don't know what I'd do without you."

"You're welcome. Just don't expect miracles. Okay?"

Elena heaved a breath. "I just shudder at the thought of what she's going through and that I might never see her again."

Tess hung her head. The situation was heartbreaking, and though she was doing her best, it simply wasn't good enough. She wasn't good enough. But what else could she possibly do?

"I can't make you any promises except this one," Tess said. "I won't stop until either Cat's safe or those responsible have paid for what they've done to her."

Throwing her arms around Tess, Elena hugged her.

"You're a good person, Tess. Your parents must be very proud."

Now it was Tess's turn to get choked up. She'd never known her mother. Or her father. And the only person who'd ever been there for her…

But this was not the time to think of what was waiting for her in Manhattan. Distractions clouded judgment and poor judgment cost lives. Focus. Focus would get the job done and see the guilty pay for their crimes.

Tess hugged Elena back. "Please, you'll have people thinking you're a rich old lesbian and I'm your gold-digging plaything."

Elena laughed. Not a gutsy belly laugh, but a laugh as refined as her English.

"You're a beautiful young woman, Tess, so don't take this the wrong way, but give me a big, fat dick any day of the week."

Tess snickered and shook her head. Such language from such a gentle soul. It always amazed Tess how people were such a constant source of joy and surprise.

"Sorry," said Elena, "did I use bad English?"

"No. No, you got your message across perfectly." She shook her head again and patted Elena on the shoulder. "Ready to get back to the search?"

"Whatever you think is best."

Tess pointed to the next street leading off the square. "That one?"

Elena nodded. "You just say. I'll follow."

Walking at Elena's pace, that of a seventy-year-old with knee trouble, it was going to take forever to get around to all the establishments they had to. Ideally, she'd have liked to have finished this morning, but that was never going to happen. It was a pity she couldn't speak Polish so she could dash around doing it at her own pace.

Probably sensing Tess was walking slowly solely for her benefit, Elena said, "We can go faster, if you like."

It was better to go slow and steady, than have to quit before they'd finished because Elena was exhausted.

Tess said, "No, this is fine."

"Tess?"

"Hmm?"

"Would you mind if I asked you about something? Not about your past, but something else."

Tess shot Elena a sideways glance. The last time the woman had framed a question like that, it had dug way too deep. "Okay," she said with a tone that meant it probably wasn't.

"How do you do what you do?"

"Do what?" asked Tess.

"Fight."

Tess had spent the best part of a decade studying the most deadly fighting arts she could find in the Far East. It was the only way she'd be able to do what needed doing back home. But she never told anyone her plan. In fact, she never told anyone anything. Information was power. The less information anyone had about her, the less power they had with which to hurt or control her.

"Like I said, I studied karate for a while. Got pretty good at it."

Elena smirked. The look said 'yeah, right' so she didn't have to.

With as innocent an expression as she could muster, Tess said, "What?"

82

"Pretty good at it. Seriously? You're forgetting I've raised a daughter around your age. Don't you think I've learned how to tell when someone is trying to pull the wool over my eyes?"

"It's true."

Elena nodded. She looked away to where a water standpipe had been opened up to gush forth a fine spray. Screaming with joy, children ran through the mist.

"It's a nice day, isn't it?" Elena said.

"Lovely."

Elena took another sip from her bottle of water. "Warm too."

"Yes."

"So why don't you take off your jacket?"

Tess stopped and slowly turned to Elena.

Elena took hold of Tess's right forearm, her fingers pressing on the eight-inch-long strip of concave steel which had been shaped to hug Tess's ulna perfectly.

Tess ripped her arm away, but knew it was already too late. Elena had discovered her body armor. An eighth of an inch thick and drilled with holes to reduce its weight and thus reduce its impact on her techniques, a strip hugged each forearm, secured inside an elasticated tube. Tess needed an edge when she faced crazed attackers armed with baseball bats and knives. Armor gave her that edge.

"I felt it when you hugged me," Elena said.

"And?"

"And someone who is only pretty good at karate doesn't wear custom-made body armor."

Tess stared deeply into Elena's tired, bloodshot eyes. It had been so long since she had shared anything with anyone, she'd almost forgotten how. Or why someone would ever want to.

The seconds crawled by in chilled silence.

Finally, Elena heaved a great breath. "I can only guess at the horrors you've known that have made you who you are, but one thing I do know for certain is this – they're in the past, gone forever. Now, you have a choice: you can either walk away and build a wonderful life, or you can let your past consume you and ruin any chance of happiness you'll ever have."

Elena meant well. But she didn't know what had happened, what Tess had been forced to endure. If she did and if she had the power to do something about it, there was no way she could ever simply turn the other cheek and let the guilty go unpunished. Having suffered what she had, how could Tess ever just get on with life as if everything was rosy?

Elena cupped Tess's cheek. "Promise me you'll think about what I've said."

Nonchalantly turning away, Elena pointed to a restaurant on the left-hand corner of the street they were heading toward. "Shall we see if this place has anything for us? I don't know about you, but I've a good feeling about this one."

Rooted to the spot, Tess watched Elena shuffle toward the restaurant. A good feeling? That was strange, because the feeling Tess was getting was worse and worse.

She was getting too close to this woman.

Too close to this problem.

She couldn't afford that.

Emotional attachment was the surest way to a bad ending. If a person had feelings for someone, they'd sacrifice for them. The more feelings they had, the bigger the sacrifice they'd make. Tess had to pull back. Had to remain detached. Had to be able to do what needed doing without having to consider how it might impact others.

It was feelings for someone that almost got her killed in Shanghai. Feelings which almost made her sacrifice what she'd spent nearly ten years planning.

Tess barely knew this woman. Had never even seen her daughter. This was a job. Not a favor for a friend. Not an obligation for a loved one. It was a job for a nobody. If it came down to it, she wouldn't be putting her life on the line for a couple of strangers. Oh, no. She had far too many plans, far too much justice to administer. After what she'd been through to get this far, there would be no sacrifices today. 'Friendship' ended here, now. She needed to stay detached. Objective. Focused.

Elena turned around and offered her bottle of water. "If you're tired, you can rest here while I go and ask."

Tess declined the water with a wave of her hand. "No, I'll come in."

She'd do what she'd promised. Then she was gone. No matter what happened. A doctor could slice away a tumor without needing to hug the patient afterward. That was why they didn't break down in tears if the patient died, but went on happily living their life.

Sacrifice? Sacrifice was for losers.

Chapter 13

THE RESTAURANT ON the corner was a bust. Just like everywhere on the first couple of streets they'd tried. A bistro just a few doors along was a bust too. And a hotel further along.

As they tramped into a hotel on the opposite side of the street with a lantern hanging over the entrance made of rose-colored glass, Tess wondered if they were ever going to find any sign Catalina had ever even been in Krakow.

It was strange they hadn't. Very strange.

Elena had been adamant that this was the right area, so how come not one single person had seen Cat?

Then it dawned on Tess.

She looked at Elena waltzing over to the reception desk in a swanky hotel with tens of tiny lights scattered across the ceiling and abstract wall hangings inspired by the works of Pollack, Monet, and Kandinsky.

Any fool could see Elena was seriously ill. But who was to say her illness was purely physical? And even if Elena's mind was as sharp as it always had been, Tess had witnessed firsthand Elena's total disregard for the effects of mixing alcohol with her medication.

"Oh, God." Tess drew her hands down her face. Her shoulders slumped as all the energy drained out of her like the sand falling through an hourglass.

In Shanghai, while she'd been recovering after the Leong incident, Sergei had persuaded her to down a few shots of vodka. Once the alcohol had mixed with her meds... Man, she could still picture Sergei's dog levitating, even though she knew it hadn't.

Maybe the reason they couldn't find Elena's daughter was that she'd either never come to Krakow with her mother or that she'd never even existed. Elena might be a kind old soul, but that didn't mean she wasn't completely whacko, living in her own drug-fueled reality.

"Oh, God, no," Tess said under her breath. That was it. That explained everything. Elena was a nutjob who'd dragged Tess into her fantasy. A kindly old thing, but completely cracked.

Tess slumped down onto a beech stool formed from a single piece of wood cut and bent into a Z shape. It was stylish, but uncomfortable. Tess didn't care. She had bigger problems than on what she was sitting.

She groaned quietly, long and slow. This was what happened when you felt sorry for people and tried to help them. That was why she had her rule. Why the hell was it so goddamn difficult to stick to it? No feelings. Ever. For anyone. It was simple enough.

Turning to the reception, Tess watched Elena gabbling on in Polish. Tess could imagine the stories she was telling the poor man in the white shirt and black tie. He'd probably been having a decent day up until now.

Tess slumped forward, dropping her head into her hands.

So what was the story this time? Maybe Catalina was a scientist who'd discovered how to turn water into gasoline and the Saudis had kidnapped her to retain their power through the world's dependence on oil.

From what appeared faraway in the distance, Tess heard a voice, but she was too deep in thought to register what was actually being said.

"Oh, Christ." Tess shook her head. What was she going to do? Okay, she'd feign a migraine. Excuse herself and head back to her hotel. By tomorrow, Elena would have dreamed up another crisis and roped in another stranger to help her solve the mystery.

That faraway voice spoke again. But this time, something clicked and Tess looked up.

Bright-eyed, Elena beckoned her.

Tess trudged over. She did not want to be dragged any deeper into this whacko's fantasyland.

Elena beamed. "Marek saw Cat."

Chapter 14

JUST LIKE THAT of a cartoon character, Tess's jaw all but hit the floor when this revelation blindsided her.

Elena continued, "Around nine twenty yesterday."

Tess heard the words, understood them perfectly, but still couldn't grasp their meaning.

"What?" Maybe she'd misheard.

Marek spoke reasonable English, but with the usual Eastern European accent which meant a lot of R rolling and guttural consonants.

"Yes," he said, "she come asking for work, but we have no work, so she go."

Tess pointed to the photo on the ebony-colored counter in front of them. "This woman? You saw this woman? Yesterday?"

"Yes, I remember because, er, well, she very pretty girl, you know."

"At nine twenty?"

"About." Marek shrugged. "I cannot be certain. Maybe, er, nine thirty."

Tess looked at Elena. The woman's drawn, gray face suddenly burst with more life, more color than Tess had ever seen.

Just as emotional involvement created problems, so too did detachment. While detachment was necessary to a degree, it had to be tempered by compassion. If Tess couldn't temper hers, she'd be just one more asshole blundering through the world, blaming everyone else for everything that was going wrong, while not contributing one damn thing to making it any better. And if there was one thing which was certain it was that the world didn't need one more asshole.

They thanked Marek and headed for the exit, Tess ambling slowly as the revelation sank in, Elena striding out as if she'd had a shot of adrenaline.

But Tess turned back. "Excuse me."

Marek looked up.

"Do you know Jacek Grabowski?"

"No. Sorry."

"That's okay. Thanks."

Outside, while Elena bounced along as if going on a first date with a man she'd had a secret crush on for years, Tess struggled with how she'd condemned Elena so easily. Guilt gnawed in her gut. Her instincts had told her Elena was good people – why the devil hadn't she listened instead of overthinking the situation? She'd have to make amends for that, or it would continue to eat away at her.

At the next place, they drew another blank, but one place after that confirmed that Cat had been there sometime between 8:45 and 9:15. As the times were getting earlier the further along the street they went, it looked like Cat had started at the end of this street and worked her way down toward the square.

They continued along the street.

At the other side of Planti Park, a small café advertising what sounded utterly revolting but probably tasted absolutely delicious – an all-day English Breakfast Fry-up – confirmed the theory. Cat had called there around 8:45.

That was the only confirmation they needed. They headed back to the main square. Cat had called her mom around 10:00. She'd obviously explored a different street between 9:30 and 10:00. If they could find which one, they'd be one huge step closer to discovering what had happened to her..

As they neared the main square once more, Elena said, "Have I said something wrong, Tess?"

"No, I, er… No."

"You're very quiet."

"Don't worry. That's just me. I suppose I'm so used to traveling alone, I've forgotten what it's like to have someone to talk to."

"Oh, thank heavens. I was starting to think I'd upset you with what I said earlier."

"No. No, it's okay. It just got me thinking about things I shouldn't. Not when I need to focus on finding Cat."

Elena covered her mouth with her hand. "Oh, I am sorry. I didn't mean to be a distraction. Please, anytime you need to, just tell me to shut the hell up – that is how you say it, isn't it – shut the hell up?"

Tess flashed her a reassuring smile. "Yes, that's how you say it. And yes, I will, don't worry."

"Good."

91

Elena took a sip of water and then offered it to Tess. She took it and shared a drink with the lady.

'Shut the hell up'. If only Tess had a switch that let her make her own mind shut the hell up.

Back in the square, Tess pointed to the next street. "Logically, Cat would've taken that one next."

"Yes, she'd have followed her plan so she didn't have to double back later to catch places she'd skipped."

"Are you still feeling okay?" Tess said. "You're not tired yet?" They'd been walking for hours, and while the pace had been gentle, they'd still been on their feet the whole time.

Slapping Tess playfully on the arm, Elena said, "Don't you start. I get enough of that from Cat."

Tess pointed to Szewska Street. "Shall we?"

With a greater sense of urgency, they marched toward Szewska. Tess could already see the first place they'd have to try – Hotel Grand Krakow.

The automatic doors opened and they walked in. The fireplace was impressive. A coat of arms carved into the stone chimney breast displayed a crown atop three towers and an eagle inside a doorway – the symbol of the city.

At the reception desk stood a snooty-looking woman with her hair in a bun.

Placing her photo of Cat on the desk, Elena launched into her spiel.

The snooty woman eyed them both up and down with a look on her face as if one of them had silently broken wind, then she said something in Polish while shaking her head.

They thanked her and left. Outside, a small café across the road with round tables on the sidewalk captured Elena's attention. Undeterred by the minor setback in the hotel, Elena was so eager to glean more insights on Cat that, without looking for traffic, she launched herself toward the café.

Zipping silently along, a group of young teenagers on Segways flew down the street straight at Elena.

Tess darted into the road. Grabbed Elena around the waist. Whisked her across to the other sidewalk as the guys sped by.

The sudden movement proved too much for Elena. She coughed. Then coughed harder. And then harder still. Tess pictured a lung flying out and landing on the sidewalk at any second.

She guided Elena over to the only free table outside the café and eased her onto one of the chrome-finish seats.

Bent over her knees, Elena shuddered as she coughed into both hands.

Tess took a fresh bottle of water out of her black backpack, opened it and offered it to Elena.

Elena tried to take it, but was coughing so much, she couldn't.

Tess held the bottle to her lips.

Elena did her best to drink but just splashed water all over the ground. She put her precious photo of Cat on the table and took hold of the bottle herself. Spluttering out as much water as she drank, she managed to down a few drops.

A gust of wind blew Cat's photo off the table. It tumbled through the air and landed under a table a few feet away. Tess turned to retrieve it, but a woman with long blond hair picked it up. However, she didn't hand it back immediately, as someone would normally do.

Instead, she glanced at it, then paused to scrutinize Elena, then glanced back to the photo, and finally passed it to Tess. The incident only lasted a moment, but it was long enough for it to be noticeable.

Tess thanked her in Polish. "Dziekuje."

The woman nodded, then returned her gaze to Elena, who appeared to have struggled through and had managed to get her coughing fit under control.

"Are you okay?" Tess held her trembling hand. "If you need to rest, we can take a taxi back to your hostel."

With the occasional splutter between words, Elena said, "But we're so close. We can't stop now. We can't."

"You're sure?"

Having a last cough, she nodded.

Tess took out her phone. "You know, if we lose this" – she held up the photo of Cat – "we're completely screwed." She placed the photo flat on the table and then took a shot of it with her phone.

The blonde woman stared. But not at Tess – at the photo on the table.

Tess took another couple of shots to be safe, then turned to the blonde. She held up her phone with Cat on it. "Excuse me, but have you seen this woman?"

The blonde said, "Przykro mi, nie mowie po angielsku."

During her time in Poland, Tess had heard that enough times to know it meant the woman didn't speak English.

However, verbal communication wasn't the only means by which to ask someone a question. She pointed at the blonde woman, then her own right eye, then to the picture of Cat, and finally, she gestured to the café.

With a smile that was as fake as her hair color, the woman shook her head and returned to texting on her phone.

"Elena, I think this woman saw Cat. Can you ask her in Polish?"

Elena started to speak, but only got a few croaky words out before the effort started her coughing again.

Tess studied at the blonde. She was a stunning woman. But there was something not quite right. It was early in the morning, when most women would look at their very best, having freshly showered, put on clean clothes, and applied fresh makeup. But this woman?

Her lemon dress was a little disheveled, not neatly pressed. Her hair cascaded over her shoulders, but lacked the body and sleekness that washing and styling would normally achieve. As for her cosmetics? That was more of a touch-up job than a fresh makeover.

The woman had either had a hot date last night and not yet made it home, or... Or she was a 'working' girl.

Of the few words Tess knew, 'please' was one of them, so she started with that and just hoped the woman actually did understand a little English, as many young Polish people seemed to do.

"Poprosze." Tess pointed at Cat again and then at Elena. "This mother, er, mom, er, er... mama. This mama. She, er... very, very sick." Tess feigned coughing and then solemnly shook her head. "Very sick. Poprosze, help mama find..." She pointed at Cat again.

Blondie looked at Tess, then slid her gaze over to Elena. The color and glow that Elena had had just moments earlier had vanished, replaced by that gray complexion and drawn skin that she'd had when Tess had first met her.

Blondie nodded to Elena. "She very sick. She will be well?"

In silence, Tess grimaced.

With a face showing absolutely no emotion, Blondie eyed Tess and then Elena again. Finally, she pointed at Cat on Tess's phone. "She have big trouble."

Elena gasped and slapped her hand over her mouth.

"So you saw her?" Tess said. "Do you know where she is now? Who took her?"

"Bad man take. Very, very bad."

Gasping again, Elena covered her face with both hands as tears welled in her eyes.

"Where?" Tess said. "Where did he take her?"

Chapter 15

BLONDIE SAID, "WHERE I don't know."

"But you know Jacek Grabowski?" asked Tess.

"Who Jacek Grabowski?"

"The man who took this woman." Tess held up the photo again.

"Is not name," said Blondie.

Goddamnit, they were getting fewer and fewer leads. When were they going to catch a break?

"Do you know why he takes women?" asked Elena.

Blondie rolled her eyes. "For candle dinner and romance."

"Oh, God, no." Tears again rolled down Elena's cheeks.

"So how long does he usually keep them?" asked Tess.

"How long? What you mean 'how long'? Forever is how long. You think this rape? No, this business."

"What?"

"Is business," said Blondie. "Beautiful woman worth big money."

Elena squealed as if someone had poked her in the side with an ice pick.

"Oh, Christ." Tess rubbed her brow.

The nightmare Tess had pictured involved either rape or murder. What the blonde was implying suggested a nightmare on a whole other level.

While prostitution was legal, kidnapping a woman and imprisoning her in a brothel certainly wasn't. At least now, if Tess wanted their help, the police would have to get involved.

"You see. Can do nothing." Blondie waved them away. "Now you know. Now you go."

Tess slapped her hand down on the table. "We're not going anywhere until we get Elena's daughter back. Will you help us?"

Blondie studied Tess, as if deciding if she could trust her.

Tess needed to secure her help – she was the best lead they had. "If you're worried about your safety, I can protect you."

Arching an eyebrow, Blondie snickered. "You?"

At five feet seven inches, Tess was taller than most women, but she could see how that alone would mean nothing to someone who hadn't seen her in action. "So the police. We can go to the police."

Blondie leaned toward Tess. "Say me. In your country, police all good and don't take money? Or sometime bad man do bad thing and police do nothing?"

Tess had no comeback for cold hard fact. The only reason organized crime existed was because the crime bosses knew exactly whose palms to grease to remain untouchable.

Blondie nodded at Tess's silence and leaned back in her chair.

Her voice wavering, Elena said something in Polish. Tears streamed down her cheeks,

Blondie looked at her coldly, but said nothing.

Tess peeled off some notes from the roll in her pocket and offered the woman two hundred zlotys. Fifty bucks seemed a fair price for a little information. "We need to find this man."

With a bored expression, Blondie raised an eyebrow at Tess again.

Altogether, Tess had around six hundred zlotys and a couple of hundred dollars she always kept on her for emergencies. The haul totaling around three hundred and fifty bucks, she bundled up all the notes and held them out to the woman.

"Here. There's nearly two thousand zlotys. It's yours."

"I sorry, but your daughter you no see again. Best you accept."

Without making any sound, Elena sobbed, her whole body juddering as if she was having a fit.

Tess could drag Blondie down an alley and beat the information out of her, or she could appeal to her compassion. While both strategies worked, the results differed person to person. The secret was in judging which strategy to use with which individual.

Tess leaned over to Blondie. "As you can tell, Elena is very sick. Every day she has to fight to stay alive. Even so, she's so sick she could die today. Or she could die tomorrow. Or, if she's really, really lucky, she could live this week, maybe even next week too, and die then. But if you don't help her find her daughter, she's going to die right this second right in front of you."

And Elena would die. Not physically. But in every other way possible.

Blondie locked eyes with Tess, then swung her attention to Elena. She huffed, then screwed up her face for a moment, obviously deep in thought.

Finally, Blondie said, "I don't know name."

"Okay, so you don't know the man's name. But you do know what he looks like, don't you?"

She shrugged the way someone shrugged when they couldn't be bothered doing something without that little bit of extra coaxing.

Tess stood and beckoned Blondie. "Come with me, please."

Blondie sighed as if this was the most uninteresting day she'd ever known, but she got up. As did Elena.

Tess led them down the street, back toward the square.

"Tess, where are we going?" asked Elena, her cheeks wet, eyes red.

"The square."

"Why? What good is that going to do?"

"You know you told me I could tell you to shut the hell up."

"Yes?"

Tess shot her a sideways glance.

"Oh. Okay. Sorry."

Back into the square, Tess turned to Blondie. With a sweep of her arm, she gestured to all the tourists and locals swarming the place. "Point to the man who looks most like the one who takes women."

Blondie frowned. "But it not right man."

"I know. Just find a man who looks like him."

Blowing out a weary breath, Blondie sauntered further into the square shaking her head. Quietly, Tess and Elena walked a few paces behind.

Turning this way and that, Blondie panned her gaze from man to man to man. After a couple of minutes, she pointed at a man standing behind an outdoor stall which burst with a rainbow of flowers. "Him. But shorter hair. Younger. Smaller nose."

Wanting to be sure, Tess pointed. "The man selling flowers?"

"Yes. I go now?"

Already walking toward the man, Tess turned back. "No. Please wait there." She pointed at Elena. "Don't let her go anywhere, Elena."

Chapter 16

TESS STUDIED THE flower seller. A very attractive man, he was forty-ish, had wavy brown hair hanging over his collar, a square-jawed face, and gentle eyes. With his business being in the main tourist area, there was a good chance he'd speak English. Checking that was the first job. And the easy part.

She sauntered over, glancing sheepishly at the gray cobbles when he caught her eye.

"Czy mowi pan po angielsku?" she asked.

He answered her question by replying in English. "Of course. Which flowers would you like, please?"

Great. That would make this a lot easier.

Tess smiled coyly. "Well… it's not really flowers I want" – she glanced down, shuffling from foot to foot – "but, er, a small favor."

"A favor?"

"My best friend at home is always teasing me because she has a handsome boyfriend and I don't."

"You don't? No!"

"I just can't find the right guy." Tess shrugged as if the situation was hopeless. "But if you don't mind me saying, you're the most handsome man I've seen in Krakow."

Feigning embarrassment, but obviously delighted, he waved his hands at her and turned away. "Please, no. Twenty years ago... hmmm... maybe."

"Really. The most handsome man I've seen."

"Then, thank you. Now, what is this favor?" He wagged his finger and laughed. "I hope not for borrow money, because rich men no sell flowers."

"No. Not money. I just want to make my friend jealous." Tess held up her phone. "Can I have a photo with you, please?"

"Just a photo? But of course."

Marching out from behind his stall, he beckoned her closer. "Come. Come."

Tess scampered over. They put their arms around each other, beamed into the lens, and Tess took a selfie.

"Oh, thank you so much."

"No, is my pleasure." He plucked a red rose from his display and handed it to her. "One beautiful flower for another."

"Oh, that's so sweet." She smiled and held up her phone again. "Okay, so one last one. Can you look serious and moody maybe?"

A hearty laugh burst out of him. Grinning, he wagged a finger at her. "Are you sure someone is not pay you for tease me?"

Tess put her hands together as if begging. "Just one. Please."

He folded his arms and adopted a stern pose.

"Oh, fantastic." Tess clicked a couple of shots. "Thank you so much. Bardzo dziekuje."

"Oh, you speak Polish! Prosze bardzo. You are very welcome." He waved as she scampered away.

Tess beckoned the other two women, who were standing, mystified. Deep in the square, Tess waited for them. The three of them together again, Tess approached the portrait artist with whom Elena had chatted earlier about creating an enlarged drawing of Cat from a photo.

"Excuse me?" Tess said.

The artist, a man with a braided beard looked up from sharpening his pencils.

"Do you speak English, please?"

He hovered his hand in the air and shook it. "Little."

Handing Elena her phone displaying the serious photo of the flower seller, Tess said, "Tell him to draw this, life size, but that we want to modify it."

"Okay." Elena talked with the man.

Tess looked to Blondie. "I want you to watch the artist and describe what needs to change to turn the flower man into the bad man. Okay?"

"You think I nothing to do better than stand all day here?"

Tess took out her wad of money again. "So, what do you want? This?"

"I want know why you think you win with bad man. Why I trust you to good do, not big trouble bring."

"Tell me what I need to know and you won't have to worry about the bad man again."

"I no worry." Blondie shook her head with a shrug. "I have manager. He rip off balls of bad man if me he try to take."

Putting her hand on Blondie's forearm, Tess said, "You help me and I'll 'rip off balls of bad man'. Today."

Blonde sniggered at Tess.

That reaction was understandable – words were easy. Tess unslung her backpack and turned away from Elena and the artist. Unzipping her bag, she crouched, then beckoned Blondie closer.

Blondie squatted in front of Tess. Between them, they shielded the bag from sight.

Opening her bag, Tess nodded to her bulletproof vest inside. "Do you know what that is?"

Blondie reached in and felt it, then nodded to herself. "Hmmm. Bullet vest." She looked up and stared into Tess's eyes, as if judging her in that very moment. Finally, she said, "You bad woman?"

Tess stared back. "An absolute nightmare."

Chapter 17

THE ARTIST LEANED back from his work, the portrait finished under Blondie's guidance. Tess took a photo of the drawing with her phone. The guy they were looking for was a remarkably handsome man. If he had the charm to match his looks, it was no wonder he could lure women into danger.

A trumpet sounded.

Tess turned to St. Mary's Church on the edge of the square. High in the tallest of the two red brick towers, the trumpeter abruptly ended his signal after only a few notes, leaving the melody unresolved. Legend said that in the thirteenth century a sentry had sounded the alarm by trumpet call, warning the town that rampaging Mongol hordes were close by. Unfortunately for him, they were far closer than he thought – an arrow hit him in the throat, cutting his warning call short. Despite that, his warning saved the town. All these centuries later, on the hour every hour, a trumpeter sounded his short call to commemorate his sacrifice.

Just as the sentry's warning had come last-minute but had still saved Krakow, so Tess hoped her call to action hadn't come too late and she'd still save Cat. She turned away from St. Mary's silent tower, praying that such a rescue would not demand the same level of sacrifice as that of the sentry.

With the picture rolled up and in a cardboard tube, they left, Blondie led the way, this time. Her attitude had changed since discovering Tess might be as bad as the bad man. Even more so after witnessing Tess's cleverness in turning a complete stranger into a fair representation of the man they were hunting. Maybe she'd started to believe Tess really could get such a dangerous man off the streets. Unfortunately, while they had a picture of him, they'd still no idea how to actually find him.

Back on the street on which they'd found her, Blondie pointed down a narrow alley which served as access to the rear of some of the buildings.

She said, "This where I see his car sometime."

Other than wheeled refuse bins, the alley was empty.

"What kind is it?" asked Tess. That wasn't helpful now, but it might be later.

Blondie didn't blink. "Mercedes S500, 4.7-liter twin-turbo V8. Black. 2015 model."

"Oh." Tess had expected a color, a reference to its size and maybe if they were really lucky, even a manufacturer. That would teach Tess for stereotyping. And it left the door open to expect even greater treasures. "I don't suppose you got a license plate?"

"What is license plate?"

"The car number." Tess pointed to a delivery truck on the street. "The number and letters on the front and back."

"Ahhh. Er... it have two and five. What else..."
She shrugged she didn't know.

That was better than nothing. "So when he's not in this part of the city, where is he?"

Blondie shook her head and shrugged again.

"Would your manager know?"

"No."

"Would any of your friends know? They must want this guy off the street as much as we do."

"Meh... Maybe. Maybe no."

"Please," said Elena, panting for breath, "time is running out for my Catalina."

Blondie held up a hand, gesturing for Elena to wait, and then took out her phone. She scrolled through her contacts.

Tess looked at Elena. The lady was slouched and gasping for air even though they were standing still.

"Do you need to rest?"

Elena shook her head. "I can rest later."

Tess pointed to the café at which they'd met Blondie. "At least sit and get your breath back while we work out where we're going next."

Gasping for air, Elena nodded and staggered a few steps toward the café.

Tess turned to Blondie, who was now talking in Polish on her phone. "We'll be outside the café."

Blondie nodded.

Fearing Elena would fall, Tess took her arm and helped her over to a chair.

"Order whatever you like." Tess reached out to put some cash on the table, but Elena caught her hand.

"I still have a little money," Elena said. "You're already doing so much."

"But I need you to translate. So eat, rest and get your strength back. It could be a long day."

"Are you eating?"

"Maybe," Tess said. "But I want to try something first."

"So, I'll wait."

Tess took out her phone and selected the cell phone number they had that belonged to the man they were hunting. Every time they'd called it, they'd gotten nothing but a ring tone. Maybe the guy screened his calls and only took those from numbers he recognized. That was fair. But maybe there was another way they could reach him.

On her phone, she attached a photo of the drawing they had of him to a text message, then handed the phone to Elena. "I need you to type something in Polish."

Taking the phone, Elena said, "Okay."

Tess dictated slowly enough for Elena to translate and type, "We know who you are. We know where you are. Release Catalina Petrescu or we're coming for you."

Elena finished typing and Tess sent the message.

The man screened calls to avoid speaking to people, but he might be curious enough to glance at a text because there was no direct interaction. That was all she needed – get his attention with a little bluff backed up with an image of him.

Elena sat up in her seat, her breathing coming a little easier. "Do you think it will work?"

"No."

"Oh." She slumped again and her expression dropped. "Then why are we doing it?"

"Like I said, it's just an idea. I don't know if it will work, but it's worth trying."

109

There was no way Cat would be released following such a simple threat. But those who had her might now keep her safer than they otherwise would because she might be of use as a bargaining chip. After all, they had no idea who had sent the text and the photo. For all they knew, it could be a much bigger gang with a lot more firepower. Keeping Cat safe was suddenly in their best interests.

Also, it might finally open the lines of communication. After seeing the photo from Tess's phone number, he might be more willing to take her call. If he did, maybe she could bluff her way into a meeting.

Tess waited a couple more minutes and then phoned the number. It rang and rang and rang..

"What's that?" Elena said, frowning.

Tess looked at her. "Hmm?"

"That. That noise."

Tess took her phone away from her ear so she could try to pick up on the sound Elena was hearing.

She listened, then walked a few paces away from the café back toward the alley where the man sometimes parked his car. The noise got louder. A phone was ringing.

Tess homed in on the sound, walking over to a green trash can on the roadside. She pawed away flyers, newspaper, fast-food packaging, bottles...

A gray plastic phone lay there. Ringing.

She picked it up. Looked at the display – her number.

"Oh, Jesus." She looked back at Elena.

"What is it?"

Tess hung her head.

"What is it?" Elena repeated, her voice wavering with worry.

"It's a burner."

"Sorry, but what is 'burner'?"

Tess held up the cheap phone. "A cheap cell phone criminals use a few times and then throw away so no one can trace them through it."

Elena cupped her hands to her face and shook her head.

Tess could imagine what she was seeing in her mind – Cat beaten, gang-raped, maybe even dead. Or pumped so full of drugs, she didn't care how many took her, but wished she was dead when she crashed down off her high.

Okay, they'd caught a break getting an image of Cat's abductor, but nearly a million people lived in the city. How the hell could they find just one of them from a drawing?

There had always been the possibility that they might find Cat dead, or never even find her at all, but Tess had always believed there was a chance she could save her. Now? Now there was no way there was going to be a happy ending to this story.

Marching toward them, Blondie waved, shouting, "I have place!"

Elena pushed up and doddered over to Blondie, moving faster than Tess had seen since they'd found confirmation Cat had been in the area.

Blondie handed her a piece of paper. "Fifteen minute ago, he here."

Tess took a corner of the paper Elena was holding and turned it so she could see, but it was handwritten Polish – utterly unintelligible.

"This place in Nova Huta," said Blondie. "Is maybe twenty minute taxi."

With a renewed sparkle in her weary eyes, Elena said, "What are we going to do now?"

"Do now?" said Blondie. "You go. You go." She waved at a taxi coming toward them, which saw her and pulled in.

Elena hugged Blondie. "Thank you so much."

"Is nothing. You go. You find."

Tess held out the wad of cash she'd promised Blondie. "Thank you."

Blondie pushed it back at Tess. She locked eyes with Tess one last time. "Be nightmare. Be very, very nightmare."

Tess and Elena got into the taxi.

Finally, they had a solid lead on finding Cat. Finally, they had a real glimmer of hope. She glanced back at Blondie watching from the curb, without whom they'd never have gotten this far.

Nightmare? Man, the scum that had Cat wouldn't believe just how much of a nightmare one woman could be.

Chapter 18

THE MAN SIPPED his coffee.

Holding a pair of pocket-sized binoculars, Tess bobbed back down beside the rear panel of a blue pickup truck which was parked in the shade of a massive apartment building.

Was that Jacek Grabowski?

She quickly scanned the building's lower windows for faces, to check they weren't being spied on themselves. Five stories of cold gray functionality over style and aesthetics, the concrete monstrosity was one of the biggest apartment buildings Tess had ever seen – it just went on and on, weaving its way along streets and around corners. Strangely, all Nova Huta's buildings had a mirror image on the opposite side of the central square, so from above, Nova Huta stood a geometric marvel.

No one peered out at them.

Tess held up her phone with the drawing of the bad man on it, then turned to Elena huddled next to her. Elena nodded. Tess nodded back.

Tess again peeked through one of the gaps in the building supplies piled in the back of the pickup.

In the sun across the street, a man wearing mirrored sunglasses lounged on a bench with a newspaper open before him. He looked remarkably like the man in their drawing. To passersby, however, he would have looked like just some guy reading a newspaper, especially as he regularly turned pages.

But he wasn't reading – the angle of his neck was all wrong. It wasn't bent for him to look directly at the pages, but bent only slightly so as to give the impression he was looking at his paper while his actual eyeline was straight over the top of it. No, he wasn't reading – he was hunting.

If a woman with a half-decent figure strolled by between the ages of sixteen and forty, he'd smile and say something to them. Most replied, but none went to sit with him, even when he beckoned.

Tess and Elena had spent nearly an hour wandering the streets, scrutinizing every man they came across, but finally they'd found him. They hoped. Yes, he looked like the drawing. But how could Tess be sure it was the right man? She didn't want to beat an innocent guy to a pulp.

Tess's heart pounded and adrenaline charged her body as mental images of the impending confrontation lit the fuse in her subconscious.

She closed her eyes for a moment and drew a long slow breath.

It wasn't time for that yet.

Now, she needed clarity. Clarity until it was time to flip the switch.

She looked at the man again, struggling to visualize what he'd look like without sunglasses hiding so much of his face.

The man took a drink from a cup of coffee he'd bought at a local café and then placed it back on the bench beside him.

Tess stared at him. Was he someone of pure evil who was currently taking a coffee break from abducting women, or was he merely an ordinary guy relaxing with a drink as he watched the world go by?

Not that that was the only problem.

If he was their target, Tess had to formulate a plan whereby they could isolate him and get the information they needed. If she attacked here, on a busy street on such a beautiful day, people would raise the alarm. When the police came, he'd have the contacts to buy his way out, while she... Hell, what hole in the ground would he ensure she was buried in?

No, they had to do this carefully. But how?

She sank back down to crouch leaning against the car.

Merely bending over, unable to crouch fully, Elena said, "So how do we do this?"

Tess slowly rubbed a hand back and forth over her lower jaw. "I'm not sure."

"Well, he's going to leave sometime, so we could just wait and see if he leads us to Cat."

"Yeah, but if he's parked nearby, we'll lose him before we can get another taxi to follow him."

"Er... we could... Hmm..." Elena scratched her head. "Well, we can't call the police because he'll just deny everything so..." She sighed. "I don't know. I really don't know. And it's killing me because we're so close now."

"Don't worry, we're going to do something; I just have to figure out what."

"But he could leave any minute."

"I know."

"So we have to do something now."

"I know."

"So what are we going to do?"

Tess snapped at her, "Elena, please. You have to let me think."

With an anxious tone, the lady muttered something in Romanian. Tess appreciated that she was frantic over what might be happening to her daughter, but they didn't have a choice but to wait – they'd get one shot at this, so they couldn't afford to blow it.

Elena peeped over the top of the car again. "Oh God, he's going to go. I know it. He's going to go." She looked down at Tess. "Please, Tess. We have to do something. Now."

Yes, they did. But what?

Chapter 19

WHILE NOVA HUTA'S buildings were overwhelmingly gray in color and style, the area's spacious tree-lined boulevards were a refreshing contrast to the Old Town's claustrophobically narrow alleys.

In the sunshine on the other side of the street, Tess skulked along the street, shoulders slumped, head hung. She drew level with the man sitting on the bench, who appeared to be reading a newspaper. She didn't even look at him, but kicked a pebble lying on the sidewalk. It skipped across the ground and into the gutter.

The man said something in Polish loud enough for her to hear.

Tess glanced over. The man looked in her direction, but she couldn't see his eyes for his mirrored sunglasses.

With a welcoming smile and tone, he said something else.

"Sorry, I don't speak Polish," she said.

"You American?"

"Yes."

"Oh, I love American. Wonderful people. Very wonderful."

Tess forced out a glum smile.

"Ohhh, but why such beautiful woman is having such sad face?"

"I, er, oh, it's okay. It doesn't matter."

He folded his newspaper and put it on the bench.

"No, no, no, matter does. Polish very warm people. We no like see sad face if we can help."

Tess rubbed her jaw, as if deep in thought. After shrugging to herself, she shuffled closer, pushing out her chest as far as she could so her black T-shirt strained over her breasts. This was another reason she dreamed of having bigger boobs – a B cup was a nice handful for a man, but on the street, you couldn't beat C cups for really grabbing a guy's attention.

"I've had my purse stolen so I have no money to get back to Krakow and no money to call my friend to come get me. I don't suppose you have a phone I could borrow, please? I promise I'll pay for the call when my friend gets here."

The man was looking for a target. There was no better way to snare him than to give him an easy one. But would he bite? Or would he smell a proverbial rat?

"Oh, is horrible story. Horrible," said the man, removing his sunglasses. "I apologize my country treat you so bad." He beckoned her. "Come, of course my phone you use."

Tess slumped with relief. "Oh, God, thank you. You're my hero."

He waved his hand at her. "Is nothing. Come." He felt each of his suit pockets. "Now, where I put phone?"

Tess bounced over. "I can't thank you enough for this. I thought I was going to be stuck here all night. Or have to walk back."

118

"No, no, no. You no worry – Michal Burakowski here now. You safe."

Michal, huh? Not Jacek. But they already knew the bad man was crafty – Blondie had told them his real name was not Jacek Grabowski. A string of aliases would be a very effective strategy to use for a criminal who wanted to work out in the open.

He pulled out a cheap-looking gray phone, exactly like the one Tess had found in the trash can outside the café.

He held out his phone. She reached to take it. But he withdrew it.

Putting his free hand to his mouth as if he'd just thought of something, he said, "Hmmm... You know, I must go Krakow today. Why I not go now and you come in my car?"

Tess made her eyes pop wider as if pleasantly surprised.

"Really?" she said. "Oh, wow, that would be great. Thank you. Er, bardzo dziekuje, Michal."

"Ohhh, you speak Polish!" He grinned, wide-eyed with surprise and pleasure.

Tess looked away coyly. "Only a few words."

"But with beautiful accent."

"Really?"

"Oh, yes. Like someone from Warszawa. Er, how you say, Warsaw."

"Really? Oh, wow."

"So" – he held up his phone in one hand and car keys in the other – "you want call or you want drive?"

"You're sure it isn't any trouble?"

"Trouble? What trouble? What better than to be drive with beautiful woman on beautiful day?"

119

"Ohhh, you're so nice."

He stood and gestured to his left. "Then we go. Come."

As they walked along the street, he told her about Nova Huta's enormous steel mill, which had once been the biggest in the world. She didn't know if that was true, but he knew how to tell a tale. She studied him. He was polite, charming, and handsome. Could he really be the evil monster she was hunting?

Some of her targets in Shanghai had outwardly appeared to be perfect gentlemen leading perfect lives. But there, she'd had time and resources to ensure she made the right decision about what to do with them. Here? She had nothing but the clawing image of the hell Cat was living.

Waltzing along, he pointed to a covered alley, a tunnel running straight through the apartment building to the other side.

"Here my car."

Parked in the shade was a black car, the badge on the hood was the unmistakable upside-down Y in a circle – a Mercedes. She checked the license plate. Sure enough, it contained a two and a five, just as Blondie had said the bad man's car did.

"Whoa!" Tess stopped dead in her tracks as if surprised. She pointed at the vehicle and grinned at him. "Now that's a car."

Okay, this guy was called Michal, whereas the one who had taken Catalina called himself Jacek, but whatever his name was, he looked like the man they were hunting and had the same make of car. Was he the guy?

Admiring the car, Tess meandered around to the rear and saw the model number on the trunk: SL500. It was the make, model and color of the one Blondie had said the bad man drove, plus it had the right numerals on the plate.

He was the guy.

"You like cars?" he said.

"I like this one."

She checked further up the secluded alley. Deserted.

She glanced behind her. No one passed by on the main street.

This was going to be the best chance she was going to get.

Sensing the impending conflict, her body reacted on autopilot. Adrenaline surged through her, filling her with so much energy she almost shook trying to restrain it, while her heart pounded like a Kodo drummer on speed.

It was always the same. No matter how many combat situations she faced, it never got any easier. In quieter moments, she prayed it never would because if it ever did, she'd have lost that one shred of humanity that kept her from turning into one of the very monsters she hunted.

It was time. Time to flip the switch.

She gasped and clutched her mouth. "Oh, no."

"Is problem?"

"There's a big scratch?"

"Scratch?" He marched toward her, frowning. "What scratch?"

Tess pulled her armored gloves out from the back of her belt and slipped them on.

Chapter 20

AS MICHAL MARCHED around the back of the car, Tess pointed to a spot low down below the right-hand rear light. "Here. It looks bad."

Michal muttered something in Polish and stooped to look.

"Where? I don't see scratch."

"Here." She pointed again.

Michal bent right over to look. Tess grabbed his head and slammed it into the trunk with a loud thunk.

He automatically flung his arms up to protect himself.

She hammered her elbow down in between his shoulder blades. He exhaled with a loud wheeze as the air was knocked out of him.

Without pausing, Tess slammed her knee up into his face, then grabbed one of his hands, and yanked it up and twisted it around into a simple wristlock. She rammed him down over the trunk of his car.

He squirmed. Groaned. But was caught fast.

"Where is Catalina Petrescu?" Tess asked.

He shouted something in Polish. From his tone, she could tell it wasn't the answer to her question.

Tess levered the wristlock harder.

Grunting, Michal grimaced, his face squashed against the car's body. Blood smeared across the paint from his broken nose.

"You're going to tell me," she said. "I don't care if I have to break—"

Singing drifted up the alley. A child's singing.

She glanced around.

A little girl with long brown hair in two pigtails skipped alongside the car. When she saw Michal's bloody face, she froze, her mouth agape.

He shouted something in Polish.

With a toss of her head, Tess gestured to the little girl for her to go the way she'd been heading. "Go."

The girl just stood gawking.

Michal shouted something in Polish again.

"Go away," Tess said with more urgency.

Still the girl remained frozen to the spot.

Twisting around, Tess shouted at the girl, "Run!"

The little girl screamed and then hightailed it down the alley shouting, "Tata! Tata! Tata!"

Tess turned her attention back to Michal, but because of the distraction of the girl, she'd unconsciously relaxed her hold on him.

As he wriggled to break free, she heard a telltale click as metal flicked into place.

He lunged at her with a switchblade.

She leapt back and the knife sliced harmlessly through the air.

When facing an armed attacker, if a person couldn't flee outright, it was rarely wise to retreat as they'd gained nothing – the attacker was still able to attack and, having seen them retreat, had had their confidence boosted. However, when facing a blade, retreat could sometimes provide more counterattack options by increasing the number of angles from which a person could strike back.

Sensing he had the upper hand, Michal smirked. He slashed again. And again.

Each time, Tess shuffled back and let the knife slice nothing but air.

Because she was acting as bait, she'd had to remove her steel forearm guards, and no matter how slimline it was, she could never have looked alluring in her bulletproof vest. All she had now was her armored gloves. While they didn't only have metal across the knuckles, but a strip down the side of the hand, plus a section across the palm, a wildly slashing blade was difficult to deflect using such tiny surface areas. No, it was best to bide her time.

There was one good thing about a confident opponent – with just a little extra boost, confidence quickly turned into overconfidence.

Michal glared at her. He felt his nose with his free hand, then looked at the blood on his fingers.

He sneered. "I going to cut you, bitch. Then I going to fuck you."

He pretended to lunge at her and then laughed. He feigned stabbing low down. Then another slash high up. He laughed again, like a playground bully enjoying tormenting a younger, smaller child.

Yes, overconfidence was a skilled fighter's best friend.

Michal stabbed at her stomach. It was sloppy, lacking the wild fury of his early attacks because he was so sure he could easily kill her.

Tess blocked his knife arm with her left forearm while her right hand darted at his throat. The arc between her thumb and forefinger smacked into his windpipe.

He gagged, his mouth dropping open and tongue distending.

Tess snaked her left hand between his knife arm and his body, levered that arm up, and clasped his shoulder – immobilizing him with an armlock.

Making him struggle for breath, Tess had shocked him out of attack mode and into survival mode. She easily swung him around and slammed him into the trunk of his car.

With his face squashed against the black metal, his breathing rasped. Blood ran down the trunk and over the Mercedes emblem.

With her free hand, she stripped the blade from his weakened grasp. She stabbed it into the top of the trunk. Left it standing there.

Hooking her free hand under his chin, she yanked around and back, cranking his neck further than it would naturally turn, the blade now in front of his face.

Michal wailed, his arm being yanked out of its socket in one direction and his head being ripped off his body in the other.

"Where is Catalina Petrescu?"

"F-f-f-fuck you!"

With his free hand splayed on the trunk, he tried to push up. He must have believed that, being a man, he'd be stronger than she was so he could break free and attack her again.

She cranked the armlock and headlock on harder, levering his bones and tendons to their breaking points.

He wailed, his handsome face so twisted he looked like a grotesque gargoyle from a church in the Old Town.

Elena poked her head around the end of the alley. Tess was in complete control, so she crept closer.

Her biceps straining, Tess said, "You're going to tell me where you took Catalina Petrescu or I'm going to rip your head clean off."

She relaxed her hold slightly, let the pain she was inflicting subside, then yanked hard again, renewing the bone-breaking agony.

Bucking to break free, he shouted, "Fuck you!"

"Wrong answer."

Tess let go of his chin. The torque on his neck made his face smash into the trunk while her armlock pinned him there still.

She grabbed the knife. Speared it down into the back of his free hand. Nailed him to the trunk.

His whole body bucked as he screeched with pain.

His eyes wide with terror, he stared at the knife sticking out of his hand and the blood running down his car.

Tess said, "Next time it goes in your goddamn eye. Now, tell me where you took her?"

He didn't so much reply as squawk, "5-2-6 Dlugie Ogrody."

Tess grabbed the handle of the knife and twisted it back and forth. The cold blade scraped against the bones in his hand.

Michal cried out, half-screaming, half-blubbering.

She eased off the knife. "What street?"

Spittle shooting from his mouth, he said, "Dlugie Ogrody, Dlugie Ogrody!"

Again, she twisted.

"What number?"

"Please! 5-2-6. Please, no more!"

Tess had to be sure he was telling the truth – increasing the level of pain while checking his answers matched was the quickest and easiest method. It had worked for Sergei in Russia and once he'd passed on how to torture someone correctly, it had worked for her in Shanghai. Although, if Michal were smart, he'd tell her the truth anyway – leading her to his accomplices for them to dispose of her would be his best option for his survival.

A man's voice boomed from behind Tess. She looked over her shoulder without releasing her grip on Michal.

A man stood at the end of the alley. As wide as a door, he was either a bodybuilder, a steroid junkie, or both. He shouted something in Polish, the little girl with pigtails clinging to his side.

Elena stepped forward and shouted back in Polish. Tess couldn't tell what she was saying, but her tone was passive, not aggressive.

The man replied, his tone more mellow. Tess heard the word 'policja'. She didn't need a Polish-English dictionary to tell her that meant he might have called the cops already. She didn't want to say anything to Elena as speaking in English could cause even more suspicion. Their only option was to get away. Fast.

Elena shouted one last thing and the man and his daughter left. She turned to Tess. "I told him the guy stole your purse."

"Did he buy it?"

"Buy it?"

"Believe it? Did he believe it or is he going to call the cops?"

"I'm not sure."

Tess had an address. She was ninety percent sure it was the right one. They had to go with it.

Keeping the knife in Michal's hand and her armlock in place, she used her free hand to pat his pockets to search him. During the search, she found two phones – a smartphone and a burner. She took both. She also pocketed his wallet – whatever money he had would come in very handy. Finally, she found his car keys.

He screamed as she pulled out the knife. She held it to his throat. His eyes so wide they were almost round, the only noise he made was from gasping for air. She then bundled him into his car's trunk.

Once she had him squashed inside, where he was in no position to be a threat, she took a plastic tie from her bag, which Elena had been looking after, and bound his wrists. The ties had proved invaluable in Shanghai, so she always kept a few with her.

His face bloody, hatred boiling in his eyes, Michal stared up at Tess. "Artur will enjoy to break you."

"Yeah, yeah. I'm sure I'm going to love him too." Tess slammed the trunk shut.

They jumped in the car, Tess in the driver's seat. After slinging her backpack and gloves onto the backseat, she fired up the car's satnav and then turned to Elena. "How do I spell 'Dlugie Ogrody'?"

Elena said, "Do you want me to type it?"

"Please." Phonetics were fine – she could repeat the words she'd heard because she'd had so much practice learning languages over the past decade – but spelling Polish words? From the language tips in her guidebook, among its other idiosyncrasies, Polish had three different forms of the letter Z. What kind of a language needed three Zs, for Christ's sake?

As Elena input the address, Tess started the engine. "You're going to have to translate the directions too."

Tess would have liked to have questioned Michal further, but time was crucial. Cat had been gone for almost a day and a half now. If she was still alive, for how much longer would that be the case? Or if she had already been 'put to work', how much longer would it be before she wished she was dead?

Chapter 21

TESS PULLED THE Mercedes into the curb in front of a grocery store with heavy-duty black metal security grilles over its windows.

The car's satnav said their destination was a hundred meters around the corner behind them. They'd driven past it once, hoping no one inside would be looking out to recognize Michal's car and raise the alarm if they saw a stranger driving it.

An old hotel in a mostly deserted building, 526 Dlugie Ogrody looked to have just a door at ground level with the actual rooms on the levels above. While she couldn't be sure because she'd been driving, it looked like the door had an intercom. That could mean she'd have to be buzzed in. Maybe even give a password. Thank God she'd kept Michal alive in the trunk.

But first, Tess needed to prepare while they were still out of sight. She reached around and then pulled her backpack from the backseat.

"How are we going to do this?" Elena asked.

"We?"

"So, you're going to take on everyone in there, find Catalina and watch him?"

Elena had a point. If entry was through using the intercom, she'd need him to speak to whoever was inside to get the door open. What would she do with him then? If Tess wasted time bundling Michal back into the trunk, the security system's automatic lock function would kick in and lock the door again before she made it back to it.

She studied Elena. Frail, sick Elena. Could she really help?

Tess removed her armor from her bag. "If he's tied up and kneeling on the floor, do you think you can guard him if you have the knife?"

"Please, I used to gut pigs when I was growing up. After what he's done, he'll be lucky if I don't slit his goddamn throat the moment I'm alone with him."

"Yeah, well don't, please. Not because he doesn't deserve it, but because we might still need information from him if anything goes wrong."

Elena frowned. "We're here now. We're going to get Cat and escape. What could go wrong?"

Tess shot her a sideways look. "That's usually what people think before they get their ass handed to them."

Pulling on her bulletproof vest, Tess said, "I'm hoping nothing will go wrong, but...." She shrugged.

"If you want me to guard him, I will, of course. Anything to help get Cat back."

Tess rolled up the legs of her jeans and then put her left foot through an elasticated tube. Once the tube was on her leg, she twisted it around until the ten-inch strip of concave steel – similar to the ones for her forearms – hugged her shin bone. She put on the shin guard for her right leg, then the guards for each forearm. Finally, she slipped on her gloves.

She was ready. Physically.

Mentally, that was another question.

Getting out of the car, Tess's heart pounded like a blacksmith's hammer beating hot iron.

She hadn't killed this year. She'd half-hoped she might not have to. Half-hoped she wouldn't encounter someone who victimized other people so much they didn't deserve to live.

Half-hoped.

Deep inside, in the part of her she knew existed, but rarely liked to acknowledge, she half-hoped she would have to kill.

Not that she got off on killing. No, it wasn't the killing she liked, but the warm glow of knowing she'd made the world one tiny bit brighter. That she'd brought relief where once was only suffering. Brought justice where once hung only abuse.

It was a sacrifice. She'd traded an ordinary life of career, family, and friends for one of pain, solitude, and danger. But then that was what life was: sacrifice. As any parent, entrepreneur or athlete would testify. The secret was to only sacrifice when you knew it would bring something of value into the world. Value was the key. Ridding the world of people who forced women into prostitution? Hell, that was one big pile of value, that was.

Walking around to the back of the car, Tess's muscles twitched with nervous energy as her adrenaline kicked in at what might be lying in wait for her in the abandoned hotel.

Resting a hand on the trunk for a moment, Tess drew a couple of long, slow breaths to combat her fight-or-flight response and, thus, calm her mind and body.

With a clear mind and a steady hand, she opened the trunk. Stared down at Michal. Pressed his own blade against his cheek just beneath his left eye.

Wincing, he tried to pull away but the trunk was too small.

"You're going to get us into 5-2-6, okay?" Tess said.

"Anything. Anything."

"If you don't do exactly as I say, I'll take your eyes. If you try to warn anyone, I'll take your life. Understand?"

"Understand, yes. I do only what you say."

She hauled him out. Cut the tie binding his hands together. Pushed him into the driver's seat. She then sat behind him and thrust the knife against his throat.

He sucked air in sharply as the cold blade touched his flesh.

"Drive us to the door," she said.

He fired up the engine. Moments later, they pulled up outside the hotel.

Tess leaned forward so she could speak right into his ear. "Remember, if anything goes wrong, the first person who dies is you."

"Please, I do everything you say. Please, no more knife."

"Keys." Tess held out her other hand.

Michal put the car keys in it.

"How many of your men are inside?" She didn't care about johns as they'd either run or hide. All she needed to know was how many guards she'd have to fight.

"Two, maybe."

"Guns?"

As if it was a preposterous idea, he said, "Guns? No!"

Two guys more than likely meant at least four. No guns meant they were probably armed. Being smart, he was playing down the threat in the hope she'd waltz in with too much confidence and get the crap kicked out of her, which would save him.

"Elena, when he speaks Polish, listen to what he says so we know he's not tricking us, and when we get inside, do what we discussed earlier. Okay?"

"Okay."

Tess shoved Michal on the side of the head. "Get out and get us in."

All three of them climbed out of the car and walked to the door, where Michal pushed a button on the brass-plated intercom and spoke in Polish.

Elena nodded that what he'd said was fine.

A buzzer sounded, Michal pulled the door open, and they went in.

Tess stared at a gloomy corridor with a filthy brown carpet and walls covered in black grime. The only way to go was forward, where a staircase climbed into the unknown.

Her heart raced. What was she going to find at the top of the stairs?

Chapter 22

TESS CREPT TOWARD the stairs and up. As she did, she drew in a deep slow breath over four seconds, held it for another four, and then exhaled slowly for four. Then repeated the process. Calming her breathing calmed her mind and her body. Not that she was superhuman. Only a complete imbecile wouldn't be afraid walking into the nightmare scenario into which she was. But while her heart hammered, it wasn't running away with itself like an untrained person's would be in this situation. Similarly, her thinking remained clear, unclouded by panic.

Her slow breathing was a simple technique she'd developed through trial and error in Shanghai. It constantly amazed her how something so simple could have such a tremendous effect in staving off panic.

And thank God it did.

Without it, making bad decisions, freezing in the face of danger, or losing her coordination through adrenaline surge would have gotten her killed more times than she could count.

Standing on the landing, halfway up the stairs, she turned back to Elena looming over Michal with the knife.

Tess had bound his hands again to be safe, but she still worried that the frail lady might not really be up to handling the job. Especially if everything went south upstairs. But it was their only choice.

She nodded again to Elena, who nodded back.

Tess turned the corner.

Ahead, steps climbed up. In the ceiling, some white tiles were skewed or had fallen down to reveal black holes with the odd cable hanging down.

Despite her breathing exercise, her heart pounded faster now that she was closer to the lurking danger. The top step lay just feet away, but she couldn't yet see over it. Anything could be lying in wait. Anything. Rabid guard dogs. Six guys with Uzis. A gang of machete-toting psychos...

She stopped.

Clarity. She needed clarity. Imagination was a wonderful tool, but if she let it run wild in times of stress, it was the easiest way to see everything she most dreaded come to life – she had to picture herself winning the coming battle and not visualize herself bloody and injured. Seeing failure in her mind was the quickest way to seeing failure manifest in reality.

She drew another slow breath. Pictured sitting on her smooth rock in her favorite spot in China's Wudang Mountains, from where she could see the early morning mist clinging to the valley bottom. Calmness. Serenity. Peace.

Then...

She flipped the switch in her mind: time to kill.

Climbing up the stairs, she peeked through the dusty bars of the balcony rail, cobwebs draped between some of them.

A fat guy with a stubbly beard stared straight at her, slouched on a green sofa next to a table smothered with crushed beer cans and squashed pizza boxes. So much for the element of surprise working in her favor.

She marched up the remaining stairs, scanning the room she was emerging into.

To her left, a shaven-headed guy sat at a reception desk playing music videos on a laptop.

Michal had said there would be two men. She was certain he'd lied. Where were all the others?

A corridor led away from this central area, doors leading off it. She imagined the doors led to the hotel's rooms, though it must have been years since it had any paying guests.

Rounding the balcony rail at the top of the stairs, she had a better angle and spotted a door behind Reception which probably led to private offices. Maybe that was where the remaining men were.

The fat guy craned his neck to look around her. He was likely wondering where Michal was.

When no one followed her up the stairs, Fatty pushed to sit up properly on the sofa from which mucky lumps of stuffing burst in various spots.

Frowning, he said something to her in Polish.

She smiled as warmly as she could and moved closer to him. Of the two men she could see, he was the main threat – the other had to move from behind the reception counter to reach her, which would take him a couple of seconds longer.

Fatty stood up. A faded black T-shirt advertised some rock band she'd never heard of. But it wasn't the picture of lightning hitting a guitar which drew her eye – the butt of a semiautomatic handgun poked out of the waistband of his jeans. From the angle of the gun, it was obvious Fatty was right-handed.

Armed and the closest, he was definitely her first target.

He spoke in Polish again.

She shrugged and ambled toward him.

He stuck his right arm out to block her with his open hand.

Tess grabbed his hand.

Twisting and bending his arm to lock the wrist, she forced it out straight.

She smashed her steel-plated forearm through his elbow with a sickening crunch.

He screeched and whipped his arm away.

Tess grabbed his gun and tossed it over the balcony rail to the lower set of steps which led down to the exit, where it would be safe, well out of reach.

Before the shaven-headed guy at Reception could draw a gun and take a shot at her, she heaved Fatty around by his disabled arm to shield her.

But Shaven Head didn't pull a gun. He grabbed a baseball bat and stormed out from the reception area, shouting in Polish.

Meanwhile, Fatty swung at her with his one good arm. In a bar brawl, such a blow could easily knock someone's teeth out, but a wild punch by an untrained fighter lacked real power, accuracy and speed – the three things a strike needed to achieve the optimum result.

In Thailand, Panom had forced her to punch a mattress fastened around a tree trunk for hours at a time, day after day, week after week. Her knuckles had bled, her wrists had swollen, her muscles had torn... But, man, had she learned how to connect.

She slipped Fatty's punch and hammered in a right body hook of her own, then a left hook to his head, and a cross to the jaw. All with maximum power. All encased in her armored gloves.

Blood running from gashes in his head, Fatty staggered back dazed and then collapsed.

Tess would've liked to have moved in and finished him, but Shaven Head was too close. He leapt at her, swinging his bat at her head.

With no chance to maneuver, all she could do was fling both arms up to block the strike. It slammed into her forearm guards. Her steel guards spread the impact load along the length of each arm, sapping the bat's bone-breaking force.

But it was still a hell of a blow − it battered Tess sideways.

She stumbled over the corner of the table and fell onto the green sofa.

Shaven Head lunged to strike again.

Sprawled over the sofa, Tess slung a pizza box into his face to give her chance to twist around. He cowered, turning away. She slammed a kick into his gut.

He staggered back, face contorted in pain, while Tess rolled off the sofa and to her feet.

She shot a glance to the door behind Reception − still firmly shut. Had no one sounded the alarm?

Shaven Head stormed at her, heaving his bat back with both hands.

Tess let him − this time she had the chance to maneuver.

As he let fly with his hunk of wood to cave in her skull, she sprang closer. So close, she was inside the swing so the bat could do nothing but harmlessly swing by behind her.

She grabbed Shaven Head's arms, pinning them.

Twisted around and bent forward.

Threw him over her shoulder.

He crashed down onto the table of beer cans and pizza boxes. The table collapsed and he hit the floor.

She stomped on his knee. He shrieked.

Tess kicked his bat away and spun around.

Wavering, Fatty clambered to his feet, still groggy from her metal punches. But he came at her again. Blood caked his face.

Tess feigned a hook to his head. When he threw his hands up to protect himself, she whipped a kick into his knee.

Fatty hobbled to one side. Trying to catch his balance, he grabbed the balcony rail to steady himself.

Tess rarely used kicks above the waist. They had proven too risky in the past – on uneven or slippery surfaces, the higher she kicked, the more likely she was to lose her balance and fall. However, on level ground with good friction, she'd sometimes risk them if the payoff was big enough.

Arcing her leg high into the air, she blasted her foot into Fatty's head. The kick pushed him backwards with such force, he toppled over the balcony rail and plummeted to the ground floor.

Meanwhile, Shaven Head was struggling up.

Tess risked a sneak peek over the balcony – Elena would stand no chance against Fatty.

The big man lay on the last few steps, his neck bent at an unnatural angle, eyes open.

She spun back to Shaven Head.

On his feet, he'd lost his main weapon so he grabbed an alternative – two broken table legs.

He winced when he put weight on the leg on which she'd stomped. But it didn't stop him coming at her. Obviously more wary this time, he didn't try to rush her like before.

He flung one piece of table leg at her.

She threw her hands up and twisted away so it missed her.

Sneakily, he took advantage of the distraction and lunged, using the splintered piece of wood as a slashing blade.

Too slow.

Tess blocked his swing. While one of her forearm guards hit his arm with such force it must have caused tissue damage, her other hand caught the piece of jagged wood, his grip on it loosened by the force of her strike.

She ripped the wood away and whipped it around in an arc. Smashed it into his temple.

For a moment, he stood frozen, the piece of wood sticking out of his head.

A drop of blood trickled down the side of his face and his eyes rolled backward in their sockets.

Then he dropped to the floor as if he was a nail that had been hit by a giant hammer.

Tess looked at the door to the private room behind Reception. Why had no one rushed out? In fact, why had no one rushed out from anywhere?

She glanced at the corridor. Why hadn't the johns and women run out screaming the moment they heard the fighting?

She crept over to the door behind Reception. Eased the handle down. Peered in.

Empty.

At one side, a dirty microwave and a battered fridge suggested it was where they prepared meals when pizza and beer became too tiresome. At the other side was a bed with all the covers heaped in a pile in the middle.

She ducked out.

Froze.

Listened.

No talking. No movement. Nothing. So strange.

She leaned over the stairwell. "Elena?"

"Yes?"

"Everything okay?"

"Yes. Shall I come up?"

"No," Tess said. "Stay where you are while I check it's safe. I'll call you when it's clear. Okay?"

"Okay."

Tess prowled across the room towards the corridor which led to the hotel's rooms. It was eerily quiet. Way too quiet. Something was wrong.

There were far fewer people here than she'd imagined there would be. Where were they all? And more to the point, where was Cat?

Chapter 23

TESS STALKED TOWARD the corridor from which ten doors led off, five on either side. All ten doors were wide open. Immediately upon entering the corridor, her mind flew back to the bus station in Bangkok and her first ever experience of the squat toilet – the stench of sweat, urine and feces hung so thick in the air she could almost shovel it out.

Fists clenched and raised before her, Tess strained to hear the tiniest of sounds, wary of a three-hundred-pound gun-toting thug leaping out at any second.

But no one leapt out.

At the first door, she hugged the wall and shot a glance inside.

Nothing.

She peered in. Then entered. The smell clawing at her.

Inside, a bed covered in a stained off-white sheet sat to one side, a grimy sink hung off the wall near the bed's foot, and a bucket sat below a window that was bricked up. Tess didn't need to look in the bucket to guess from where the stench was coming.

As the clues slotted into place, horrific images formed in Tess's mind of what might have been going on here. She turned and crept across the corridor and entered the room opposite, praying she was wrong.

She wasn't.

"Oh, Christ, no." The same basic setup confirmed her suspicions. This was worse than she'd thought. A million times worse. This was no brothel and Cat's abduction was no kidnapping.

Tess shook her head. "Not this. Please not this."

An aching void raked at her gut from the inside, as if Shaven Head were carving out her innards with the splintered piece of wood.

Oh, God, how would she tell Elena?

This... This was human trafficking. At least in a kidnapping situation, there was a chance you could pay a ransom to get your loved one back. Even in enforced prostitution, there was a chance you could break in and rescue them. But this...

There was no ransom to pay. No rescue to be launched. Your loved one might as well be dead. And probably wished they were.

To be certain, Tess worked her way up the corridor and looked in all the rooms. In the room at the end on the left, she caught a glimpse of something from the corner of her eye. She strode in, reached down, and picked something up off the floor. In a little transparent plastic envelope was a four-leaf clover.

"Oh, God." Cat had been here. But Tess had been too late to save her. In the day and a half since Cat had disappeared, these monsters could have taken her anywhere. Right this second, she could be being raped almost anywhere in the world – China, the Middle East, Brazil. Even the USA.

Tess slumped, rubbing her brow. How the devil was she going to break it to Elena?

In the back of her mind, Tess heard coughing coming from way back in the hotel. She was so deep in thought about how Cat would be suffering and how Elena would take the news, that the sound didn't register at first.

The coughing got worse, really starting to hack.

Something clicked. Tess gasped. "Elena."

She made for the door.

A woman's scream slammed into Tess like a heavyweight boxer's right hook.

Tess flew down the corridor and across the room. Instead of dashing around the balcony rail and to the top to the stairs, she leapt over the rail. Using her hands and feet to absorb her momentum, she hit the wall opposite and sprang away and down onto the halfway landing.

Elena was curled up on the floor, spluttering.

Fatty was sprawled out on the floor, dead.

Michal – their only lead to finding Cat – was gone.

Tess jumped over Fatty's unmoving body and darted to Elena, where she crouched and cradled the fragile lady.

"Are you okay?" Tess asked. "Has he hurt you?"

Elena looked up in Tess's face with bloodshot eyes. Her voice croaked as she spluttered out just one word. "Ca-Catalina?"

Tess took a deep breath. "She's… she's not here."

Elena's face screwed up like the palm of an aged boxing glove.

Tess dabbed blood from her mouth where she'd obviously been hit.

Elena's chin trembling and her voice wavering, she said, "He hit me whi-while I was coughing." She gripped Tess's arm. "G-go. F-find him."

"You're okay?"

She squeezed Tess's arm harder. "Go."

Tess pulled away, but Elena didn't let go. "What is it?" Tess asked.

"I'm sorry."

"It's okay. It's not your fault."

"You don't" – she gasped for air – "you don't understand."

Tess frowned. "What? What is it?"

The lady's face screwed up again. "He ha-has the gun."

Tess glanced over at Fatty. She'd lobbed the gun down here believing it was the safest place for it. And it would have been if Elena hadn't had another of her coughing fits. Now, the one person who could lead them to Cat was armed and on the run.

Tess leapt to her feet, ripped open the door and shot out. She scanned up the street. Nothing. Down the street?

There!

Because his hands were still tied in front of him, Michal was running down the sidewalk with his shoulders swinging wildly.

Tess jumped into the car. The engine roared and she took off after him.

But Michal must have recognized the sound of his car's engine.

146

Turning while still running, he raised his gun. He blasted a shot in her direction.

She ducked down in the car, only for the wild shot to fly wide.

Tess tore down the road.

Michal made a break for the other side of the street. Tess could see a shadowy alleyway. If he made it in there, she'd have to chase him on foot. She didn't want that. Not when he had a gun.

She hit the gas.

Obviously realizing he wasn't going to make it across the wide road before she plowed into him, Michal stopped. He raised his gun. Took his time to aim.

Every fiber of Tess's being screamed at her to yank on the wheel and turn away from danger, away from almost certain death.

But calm logic overruling her primitive instincts, she steered straight for him.

He blasted with the gun. Shots tore into the side mirror, into the hood, into the windshield.

Tess leaned over to the right to hide as much as she could behind the dash. She only needed a second more.

Almost on him, she hammered on the brakes, yanked the steering wheel right, and rammed her door open partway.

As the big black Mercedes screeched past Michal, the acutely angled door caught him. Instead of splattering him like a brick hitting an overripe tomato, the angled door spun him away. He reeled across the road like a drunken ballerina and crashed into the gutter.

Even before the car stopped, Tess twisted around in the driver's seat.

A body lay in the gutter.

Oh God, please don't say she'd killed him.

Dotted along the sidewalk, a number of cowering bystanders dared to stand up and look to see if it was once more safe to get on with their lives.

It wouldn't be long before some Good Samaritan phoned the police. She had to act fast.

Tess slammed the car into reverse, shot back up the street, and stopped beside the body.

She prayed he was still breathing. If he wasn't, she'd just killed any chance of finding Cat.

Chapter 24

TESS DROVE INTO a makeshift parking lot created on the site of a demolished building, the car bouncing over potholes and rubble embedded in the ground. Parked as close to a nearby construction site as possible, she got out. A bulldozer rumbled by at the other side of a chain-link fence and two workmen used pneumatic drills in the distance.

She opened the trunk. Squashed inside lay Michal, battered and bloodied. A jagged piece of tibia protruded through a blood-soaked tear in his beautifully tailored trousers.

She'd tried to get the information she needed once. And failed. Now, she had a more secluded spot, so she could offer a little more persuasion.

Tess grabbed his ankle and twisted.

The tip of broken bone moved.

Michal screamed, though Tess barely heard it over the construction machinery.

"Give me those names," Tess shouted. "Or I'll tear this leg clean off."

Seven minutes later, Tess squashed up next to Elena in a grubby cubicle in the Internet café around the corner. She scrutinized the list of six names she'd pried out of Michal and then booted up the laptop she'd taken which Shaven Head had been using in the hotel. Unfortunately, before she'd been able to get her hands on it, the laptop had gone into hibernation mode and now required a password to access it.

This was their last hope. She had to crack it.

Michal was only the face of the gang, only the person who lured women to their lair, so he only had sketchy information on where the women went once they left the hotel. None of it anything they could follow up. He didn't even have a password for the computer – Tess had twisted his leg hard enough to know he was telling the truth there.

In the Username field, Tess input 'Artur', the first name on her list, and then in the Password field, she typed the word 'haslo' – the word for 'password' in Polish, which Elena had provided. The laptop rejected the login.

She replaced 'haslo' with 'password'.

Again, it was rejected.

Finally, she tried a third password option: 123456.

Rejected.

Tess sighed. Around the globe, countless hackers hacked countless computers with ease. Unfortunately, this beginner's technique was the only one she knew. Statistics said of one hundred people's logins, this strategy would crack at least one of them because so many people thought it was a brilliant idea to use such passwords.

But Tess didn't have one hundred people, only six. The odds were not on her side. But then they never were.

She'd often dreamed of finding someone with true hacking skills because they would be incredibly useful when she started her search back in Manhattan, but how could she find someone like that? If she approached the wrong person, she could easily find the very skills she dreamed of working for her being used to rip apart her bank account, her ID, hell, her entire life.

Okay, that was only one name down. She still had five other chances to crack the laptop. It was not the time to be despondent. Yet.

She tried the next name – Kuba – with the same three passwords.

Rejected.

She drummed her fingers on the desk, scouring the far recesses of her mind for something she might have forgotten about cracking logins. This had to work. If it didn't, they were completely screwed.

With forced cheerfulness, Elena said, "The third time's a charm."

"Let's hope so." Elena's English was amazing. Tess would have to ask her about it if ever they had a relaxed moment.

Tess input the details.

Elena gripped Tess's arm as she hit Enter.

All three password variations were rejected. And Elena's grip on Tess's arm tightened.

The fourth one was rejected too.

When 'Mateusz', the fifth name, and 'haslo' were rejected, Elena turned away. "I can't look."

Tess changed 'haslo' for '123456' and hit Enter. She gasped.

Elena snapped back around to look. She gasped too as a desktop opened up before them. Everything on it was in Polish.

"Can you use a computer?" Tess asked.

Elena laughed and playfully punched Tess on the arm. "I'm sick, not old."

She angled the laptop so she could use the keyboard. A moment later, she had a list of the most recently opened documents and was combing through them.

This time the third one really was a charm – Elena translated it as she read it, describing details of a consignment and the ship on which it sailed at midnight from Gdansk.

Elena stared at the screen, hands cupped over her mouth, eyes wide.

"Oh, God. Is Gdansk far?" Tess asked. Every time they thought they'd made headway and might have found a way to reach Cat, things got ten times worse.

Her voice wavering, Elena said, "It's a port right up in the north, at the other end of the country."

"Oh, Jesus." So there was no way they could drive. "Can we fly?"

Elena hit keys. Searched. Scanned the page. Elena sat bolt upright and leaned closer to the screen. "Yes."

"Fantastic. What time is the next flight?"

"Four twenty. What time is it now?"

Tess looked at her watch. She heaved out a breath. "Four forty-five. What time's the next one?"

Elena slumped over the desk and wept.

Tess pulled the laptop back around in front of her. The next flight was tomorrow. She heaved another breath and put her arm around Elena's shoulders.

"I'm so sorry, Elena."

"I-I... I just" – she struggled to get the words out – "w-wanted t-to hold her one las-last time."

They'd been so close to rescuing Cat. How could they have got so close only to fail? How was that fair? Well, it was as fair as a beautiful person like Elena getting a terminal disease decades before her time.

"Just a minute." Tess typed info into the search box and scanned the results. "It's around an eight-hour drive from here."

"Eight hours? It's nearly five o'clock already. We'll never make it before midnight."

"We've got satnav. If we drive like hell, we might. It's not like we have any other choice."

Elena held an open hand up to Tess. "Wait."

She grabbed the laptop.

Typed furiously.

Gasped again when she saw the results. For the first time in hours, she smiled.

"What is it?" Tess asked. "What have you found?"

Pointing at the screen, Elena said, "We can fly to Warsaw and get a connection. We can be there in around four hours."

Elena pushed up to leave.

Tess grabbed her arm. "Whoa, sit down."

"We've got to go. The plane is in an hour."

"All the more reason to buy tickets online to avoid lines at the airport."

Tess booked two flights: the 17:55 flight, which arrived in Warsaw just fifty minutes later and then the 19:40 to Gdansk, which took around the same length of time. If all went according to plan, they could be at the shipyard a little after 9:00 p.m.

153

Now they had just thirty minutes to cover the seventeen kilometers to the airport before the gate closed at 5:25 p.m. Unfortunately, rush hour traffic in Poland's second city was a killer.

Following the satnav, Tess drove as fast as she dared, but never exceeded the speed limit. The delay in getting pulled over would make them miss their flight. And if the cop who stopped them was so curious about the bullet hole in the windshield he asked to look in the trunk... Well, they'd likely be delayed by the Polish constabulary for more than just a few minutes.

Tess zipped in and out of the traffic, always below the speed limit, always signaling. Beside her, Elena gripped the dash, her knuckles white with worry. But progress was so slow it was like waltzing in mud.

Elena pointed to an opening in the next lane. "Quick, Tess."

Tess checked her mirrors, hit the gas, and darted into the space. They cruised past a few vehicles, but nowhere near fast enough.

Flying toward the next set of lights, Elena again pointed. "There!"

"Seen it." Tess zipped back into their original lane and roared toward the next set of lights.

"Oh, no, they're going to change. They're going to change." Elena covered her face with her hands.

Tess ached to floor the gas pedal and tear through the lights, but resisted. It was so hard, it was almost painful. But if they were pulled over, she'd as good as killed Cat.

"Oh God, oh God, oh God." Elena peeked from between her fingers.

Tess cruised through the lights.

"Oh, thank God." Elena panted for air as if she'd sprinted through the lights herself.

Unfortunately, no sooner were they through one set of lights than another loomed before them. All the cars ahead braked for a red stoplight.

Instead of racing to get to the lights as quickly as possible, Tess eased off the gas.

Elena spun to her. "What's wrong? Why are we slowing down?"

Tess pointed at the clock in the dash: 5:22, thirty-three minutes before their flight.

Wide-eyed, Elena stared at her. "But—"

Shoulders slumped, Tess said, "We can't make it."

"But—"

"I'm sorry. We can't." She pointed to the lines of slowing traffic in front of them. Boarding ended thirty minutes before a flight – there was no way they could be seated on the plane in the next three minutes. And once that cabin door was closed, there was no way it would open again for two late passengers.

Elena crumpled in her seat.

"What time is the next flight?" Tess asked.

With an expression like she was attending a funeral, Elena shrugged.

"Hey, don't lose hope now." Tess squeezed her hand for a moment. "We can still drive, if we have to."

"An eight-hour drive in six hours?"

A frantic six-hour drive and then a fight to the death with armed men? Yep, things were just getting better and better. But maybe they could avoid that.

Tess said, "Get my phone from my bag in the back and call the airline. There must be another flight. And check Michal's wallet. See how much money we have."

155

Giving Elena something to do would momentarily distract her from the nightmare she was living, while also uncovering their options.

Having searched the wallet, Elena said, "1400 zloty and a driving license in the name of Piotr Zemekis."

"That's around four hundred bucks. Good. That'll be useful."

"And Piotr?" Elena asked. "What are we going to do about him?"

"What do you want to do about him?" Tess asked.

"Gut him. Like a pig."

It was easy for Elena to say she was going to kill Michal. Hell, she probably even believed it herself. But when it came down to it, most people didn't have the will to end someone, no matter what crime they'd committed. No, it took a particular kind of person to kill. Even in exceptional circumstances.

A signpost for Krakow airport reared on their right. Tess changed lanes for the exit.

Elena was about to discover just how far she'd go to claim payback for those she loved. Would she be able to live with the decision she made?

Turning for the airport parking lot, Tess said, "Whatever we're going to do, it's nearly time to do it."

"I've told you what we're going to do."

"Are you sure? It's a lot harder than you think to kill someone."

"You just watch me."

Chapter 25

TESS SURVEYED THE sixth floor of the seven-level parking garage opposite Terminal 1. Everywhere was gray concrete, while in the distance, tires screeched as a driver took a corner too tightly.

Two spaces over from the Mercedes sat a red SUV, while opposite were three free spaces, then a concrete pillar on one side and a red sedan on the other. She'd reversed into a space in one of the furthest spots from the elevators to minimize the chances of passersby hearing Michal, or Jacek, or Piotr or whatever his goddamn name was.

"So you've never been arrested?" Tess asked Elena as they climbed out of the car.

"Do I look like a criminal?"

"So the police don't have your fingerprints?"

"No."

If they hadn't been so desperate to reach the airport, Tess would have dumped the car somewhere secluded and then taken a taxi. Now she had the problem of what to do with it.

Tess had worn her gloves all the time since meeting Michal. DNA evidence was another story. She could torch the car, but that might prompt a terrorist alert and shut down the airport. No, she'd have to leave the car intact. But Michal? How intact should she leave him?

Standing between the gray water-stained concrete wall and the Mercedes, Tess opened the trunk.

Michal stared up wide-eyed, his face as drawn and lifeless as Elena's from shock and blood loss.

Tess offered Elena the knife.

Anxiety creasing her face, Elena looked at her, then the knife, then Michal. Her trembling hand reached for the weapon.

Michal's eyes widened even more. Tess had gagged him with some of the gray stuffing from the hotel's sofa, so he made urgent grunting noises as the knife glinted in the shadowy light of the parking garage.

But Elena's hand stopped short of the hilt.

"You wanted to gut a pig." Tess pushed the blade closer to her.

With a heavy frown, Elena shrank back. Her mouth fell open, but no words in any language came out.

"Yours isn't the only daughter he's taken," Tess said. "And if you don't do this, it won't be the last. People like this don't change."

Shaking her head just barely, Elena finally found the power of speech. "No. No, I can't. We can't."

"And if we don't and he manages to contact his gang so they're waiting for us all armed to the teeth?"

If Tess allowed Michal to live, that decision wouldn't just kill Cat, it would probably kill her and Elena too. She pushed the knife against Elena's hand.

Shaking his head at Elena, Michal squealed like a cornered rat. He pushed further into the trunk as if a secret door might open and let him escape.

Elena jerked her hands out wide, away from the knife. "No. It's not right."

Tess stared at her. "It's okay," she said with a calm reassuring tone. "Most people can't kill. Even for the best of reasons."

Elena reached out and eased the trunk lid down. "Let God decide. If it's meant to be, he'll bleed to death."

"God isn't watching." Tess caught the trunk before it shut. "If he was, you'd be happy and healthy in Romania with Cat."

Tess pushed the trunk lid back up. She stabbed the knife through Michal's left eye right up to the hilt. Blood spurted over her hand.

Elena lurched forward and vomited onto the oil-stained ground.

Tess wiped the blood on Michal's blue jacket and then slammed the trunk shut. "We have to go."

She put her arm around Elena but the lady yelped as if Tess had burned her and pulled away. She glowered at Tess as if it were Tess who was the monster.

Tess strolled toward the elevator. It wasn't the first time someone had looked at her like that. And she'd bet it would not be the last. However, this tiny part of the world was one tiny bit safer because of what she'd just done. She'd sleep soundly on the plane. No regrets. No guilt. No bad dreams.

She turned back.

Elena was still slumped against the wall, looking even more unwell than usual.

Tess called out, "If we miss this plane, it's all over."

159

Chapter 26

IN THE ELEVATOR, Tess stuck her thumb to the Door Open button while Elena toddled over and in. The lady stood in the furthest corner away from her.

Elena had phoned LOT, the main Polish airline, from the car. There was a flight at 19:20 and a connection at 21:10. If all went well, they'd be dockside around 11:00 p.m. – just one hour to find and save Cat before the ship sailed.

Sighing, Tess slumped forward and rested her forehead against the stainless steel elevator wall.

Surely, Elena didn't think she enjoyed killing. Surely. So what had she thought they were going to do with Michal? Hand him over to the authorities for 'justice' to prevail? For rehabilitation to turn a psychopath into a caring human being?

Yeah, right, because that always worked out just fine.

It was as if Elena believed that somehow everyone was going to come through this and live happily ever after. Everyone. But how could they? Elena knew what Michal had done. Knew what his gang was still doing.

They had to pay. This wasn't a game; this was a war. A war innocent people were losing.

Tess pressed the button for the ground level. This was going to be an even longer night than she'd thought it was going to be.

As Tess strode along the asphalt path to the terminal between two small areas of neatly mown grass, Elena trudged along a few yards behind.

A cough broke the icy silence.

Then another.

Knowing what was coming, Tess turned and unslung her backpack. She scurried back as Elena bent double, holding on to a gray metal handrail, all but spluttering her lungs out onto the grass.

Tess offered her a fresh bottle of water.

Elena shoved her away.

During her training, Tess had been pummeled by kickboxers, slammed into the ground by jiu jitsu experts, and battered senseless by kung fu masters, but that shove... That shove hurt more than any beating she'd taken anywhere.

"Elena, for God's sake, I can't do this alone. I don't know Poland and I don't know Polish. If you don't help me, I can't save Cat."

Something must have clicked, because Elena's hand snaked out and grabbed the air for the bottle. Tess put it in her hand. Sipping the water in between coughs, Elena barked less and, little by little, her fit subsided.

Placing the palm of her hand on Elena's back, Tess gently rubbed. "You know I had to do that."

Breathing hard, leaning on the rail, Elena glared at her from the corner of her eye. Sweat beaded on her face.

"How many more lives would he have ruined?" Tess asked.

Elena pushed up. She handed the bottle back and then staggered on. "Are you coming?"

Okay, they were talking. That was a start. Tess caught up and walked alongside.

In the airport, they paid for their flight tickets with Michal's money, then Tess withdrew another five hundred dollars in zlotys from the ATM. She'd no idea how they were going to gain access to the dock, so it was best to be prepared with a decent bribe if they needed it.

They bought a bottle of fresh orange juice and a sandwich each, and then found a secluded spot in which to sit not too far from the gate where huge windows overlooked the runway.

The airport offered free Wi-Fi for one hour per user, so Tess fired up the laptop from the hotel. Not only did she need more information, she needed to build bridges.

She tore off a hunk of her sandwich and munched a mouthful of cardboard-like cheese, rubbery ham and limp lettuce. Not having eaten since breakfast, she barely chewed it before devouring another hunk.

"Do you have the list of names, please?" Tess asked.

Elena took it from her purse and handed it over.

She watched Tess surf to Facebook and type in the first name: Artur Bartosz. A list of users with that name appeared.

"What are you doing?" Elena asked.

That was the first brick laid in the first bridge. "I want to put faces to the names, so if we see them, we know we've found them."

Elena nodded and leaned closer.

That was a second brick.

They went through the six-name list, filtering it by Krakow and the surrounding towns, Elena providing translations, suggestions and opinions.

After forty-five minutes of searching and cross-referencing, they had found the pages of possibly five of the six names, one of which Tess was certain about because it was Shaven Head. He'd led her to the redheaded Artur Bartosz. With a grizzled face that made him look like an old seadog, Artur appeared in the galleries of three of the other names.

Tess chose the best portrait of each of the five men and photographed it to keep on her phone. She closed the laptop, which looked a decent piece of gear. She'd sell it when all this was over to help cover her costs.

"Is there anything else we can do?" Elena asked.

Tess stared into space. After the problem in the parking lot, was Elena going to be able to handle what was to come? She placed her hand on Elena's. "Only to prepare for the difficult things we're going to have to do."

Elena hung her head and gazed at the floor.

"I'm sorry," Tess said, "but it's only going to get worse."

Elena nodded, but remained silent.

"If I could do it alone," Tess said. "I—"

The lady squeezed Tess's hand. "I know you would. It's just... I've never..." She huffed and stared at the floor as if struggling to find the words to express herself clearly. Turning to Tess, she said, "How do you do it?"

"Where's Cat's father?" Tess asked.

Looking thrown, Elena said, "Er… He, er, he died in a car accident when Cat was eight. He was Canadian – why I speak English."

"And you loved him?"

"I miss him every day."

Tess nodded. "So you've raised Cat all these years on your own? You must love her too."

"Of course, but what—"

"Over her lifetime, a woman is many things, not least a lover and a mother. But she's never the two at the same time. It's as if she has a switch she can flip when she needs to be one or the other, but the switch won't let her be both at the same time." Tess shrugged. "I have a switch."

"What do you mean?"

Tess toyed with her bottle of juice. "I was like you once – just a normal person living a normal life."

"What happened?"

Tess hung her head and stared at the floor, trying to block out the images of blood. So much blood. She heaved a breath. Some things were too personal to share, too painful to even think about, let alone talk about.

"What always happens – life happened. It would be nice to go back to being normal one day, but..."

If that day ever came, Tess knew exactly where she would go and exactly what she would do there. Other than seeing justice done in Manhattan, it was the last dream to which she still clung. However, deep down, she doubted she'd live long enough for it to become a reality, but it was a pleasant distraction from the darkness that engulfed so much of her life.

"Anyway, in the meantime," Tess said, "I have a switch I can flip. It lets me do the things I do and still look in the mirror without wanting to slit my wrists."

"But why do you do them? Why don't you go and find that life now?"

Tess turned and stared into Elena's eyes. "And who'd save Cat? Who'd save all the other innocent people who are abused by monsters everywhere I go?"

"Tess, you can't change the whole world."

"No. But I can change tiny bits of it and then sleep soundly at night knowing I have."

Elena stared at Tess with such sadness in her eyes. She cupped Tess's hands. "Oh, Tess, that's not living."

"So what should I do? Dream of kids and malls and job promotions? Or of saving Cat?"

It was an impossible question to answer.

Tears welled in Elena's eyes. Tess doubted they were for Cat, this time. Now the lady saw Tess's dilemma – she had the choice either to help people in desperate need or to live a normal life, but not both.

Over the speaker system, a woman announced something in Polish.

"This is our flight," Elena said.

They ambled toward the gate.

"So that's why you travel," asked Elena, "why you have your armor? So you can help people?"

"Kind of." She'd had to check her backpack containing her armor to avoid being detained when they went through the security check, but she never went anywhere without it. Even with all her years of training, the simple truth was she was physically smaller and weaker than the average man. Her armor was a wonderful equalizer. And then some.

"But don't you get afraid?" asked Elena.

Tess snickered. It was a ridiculous question, but she couldn't blame Elena for thinking she might be superhuman. "Of course I do. Only a fool would say they didn't. The secret is in knowing how to use that fear to help you, instead of letting it paralyze you."

"You can do that?"

"You can if you've got four months to spend on an ashram in India."

"And that's where you learned about your switch?"

"No, that was five months on a mountain in China."

Tess had spent the best part of a year learning to use her mind with the same disciplined fluidity with which she used her body. But it still wasn't easy. Strangely, inner calmness required tremendous struggle.

Puffing out her cheeks, Elena blew out a breath. "Is there nothing you haven't done?"

Standing behind a bald man in a dark suit talking Polish on his phone, they joined a line of people waiting at the gate as airline staff checked boarding passes one by one.

Tess rubbed her chin. She didn't want to build up her friend's hopes, but... "You know, some of the meditation and self-hypnosis techniques I've learned can help with illnesses."

Elena forced a smile. Tess knew what she was thinking.

"Twenty years ago," Tess said, "Western doctors thought alternative medicine was complete bull. Now it's practiced in half the hospitals in the US. You might be surprised at what my methods can do."

Elena waved a hand at Tess. "Thank you, but I doubt anything can help now."

"So why are you going to England? I thought it was for some kind of special treatment."

"Compared to the Romanian health service, any treatment is special treatment. Unless you've got the money to bribe the doctors to get what you need, of course."

"What?" Tess said, stunned. "You have to bribe your doctors?"

"It's not their fault. They have to bribe their management to get promotions. And it's not like they get paid a lot to start with."

"So doctors aren't valued?"

"Catalina was paid around two hundred dollars per month. Is that valued?" Elena said.

"Whoa, Cat is a doctor?"

"Didn't I say?"

"No," said Tess. "Jesus, two hundred bucks a month?" She shook her head. "Hell."

"That's why we were going to England."

"So it's not to get you treatment?"

"Making Cat believe it was was the only way I could convince her to go. You see, no matter how grown-up they are, you always want the best for your children, and I wanted her to have the life she deserved."

Tess hung her head. When she looked up, she said, "So there's really nothing they can do?"

Elena smiled the saddest smile Tess had ever seen.

Parents sacrificed for their children. Constantly. Tess witnessed it everywhere she went. Children never appreciated just how much until they grew up and had kids of their own. But to leave your home, and all your friends and relatives, and then to die in a strange country all so you could try to give your child a better future... Man, that was one hell of an act of love.

Tess smiled back at Elena. This devoted mother would see her daughter again. Tess would see to that. See to it if it killed her.

Chapter 27

TESS AND ELENA each showed their boarding pass at the gate and were ushered into the cream-colored air bridge. Its floor gave slightly as Tess walked on it.

Tess never accepted defeat – she would not let Elena either. "You know, my techniques really might help."

"Maybe for some things."

"You've seen what I can do. That's not just a physical thing, you know – there's a huge mental aspect. I couldn't do what I do without training my mind as much as I've trained my body."

They rounded a bend in the air bridge and the open aircraft door came into sight.

Elena grabbed Tess's arm. "Can your techniques do anything for a fear of flying?"

"You don't like flying?"

Elena shot her a sideways glance.

"So what do you usually do? Take sedatives?"

"Usually? Do you think I'd be doing this if Cat's life didn't depend on it?"

As they neared the doorway, Elena glared at the plane, her face even more drawn than usual. "Oh, God… Oh, God."

Tess put her arm around her. "It's okay. I'm here."

As she stepped over the threshold into the plane, Elena muttered in Romanian and gripped Tess's arm, sinking her fingernails into the flesh.

Tottering down the aisle between the seats, Elena said, "Oh God, Cat will never believe I've done this."

Tess guided her to her seat. The easiest way to help Elena was to distract her, so she took out her phone.

"I'm going to take a photo for you to show Cat that you managed to get on a plane."

"Then you better be quick," Elena said, "because we haven't taken off yet and that door is still open."

Tess laughed, though the look on Elena's face suggested it wasn't a joke.

Tess held her phone up and took a selfie of them both, then showed it to Elena.

Elena cracked a smile as feeble as she was. "But Cat still won't believe it."

"I could teach you a meditation technique to take your mind off flying, if you like," Tess said.

Patting Tess's arm, Elena said, "If you don't mind, I'd rather just shut my eyes and try to sleep through the whole thing."

Tess could help Elena. And not just with the flight. When this was over and they had Cat back, she'd teach Elena some of the techniques she'd mastered and make sure Cat forced her to practice them. They wouldn't cure her, but they would make what time she had left more pleasant. And might even extend it.

With her eyes still shut, Elena said, "It's very freeing, you know, knowing what's going to kill you and roughly when it's going to do it. I'm lucky in a way. I bet there's no one else on this plane who knows what's in store for them, but I bet every single one worries about it from time to time. We all get so wound up about life, about what to do, what not to do, about what might happen, what might not happen, and yet, ninety-nine percent of it doesn't truly matter one scrap."

Without looking, Elena patted Tess's thigh. "Thank you, Tess. I never imagined anyone would care so much about a complete stranger to do what you're doing."

"You're welcome."

Could someone with a terminal illness be lucky? Maybe. Elena was right – it would be very freeing.

Tess fastened her belt and sank back into her seat. It was only a short flight, but it would be nearly an hour in which she could meditate to recharge her batteries. She closed her eyes, but couldn't settle – the conversation they'd had at the gate about how she did what she did clawed at her, like a child picking at a scab.

Tess wasn't a killer. In just the same way that breastfeeding a child or banging a guy couldn't define her, so neither could ending someone. A single word could never encompass what she brought to the world. Let alone what she had to sacrifice to do it.

No, she wasn't a killer. She was a woman doing what was right for no other reason than because she could. A woman with a switch. A woman who made the world a better place.

But in Gdansk, when she flipped that switch again, how many people would die?

Chapter 28

SPEEDING THROUGH GDANSK in the back of a taxi, Tess twisted her bulletproof vest back into position, it having ridden up under her clothes. She'd put it on in the airport restroom, once her backpack had finally appeared on the luggage carousel. In a little over an hour, the ship would sail to God knew where, and any chance of finding Cat would be lost forever.

Twisting her left forearm guard into place, she peered out of her taxi window.

A cream-and-red tram rattled past down the middle of the road heading into the center of Gdansk. They passed a gas station and more scrub land came into view. In the distance, silhouetted by the moon, massive cranes reared into the night sky like the skeletons of giant dinosaurs.

She'd have liked to have toured Gdansk, the birthplace of Solidarity. The struggle of a group of people fighting for the oppressed resonated with her. That movement had helped to free Poland from the communist dictatorship of Moscow and sparked the end of the Eastern Bloc. She'd never have impact on a global scale like that, but by helping people like Elena, she changed the world in her own way.

The taxi stopped at the main entrance to Gdansk's smallest port. Did the traffickers believe a small port would attract less scrutiny than a big one? If they did and they were right, that could help in the rescue too – security might not be so tight.

Tess clambered out of the taxi.

If she had been alone, she'd have sneaked into the port, just a shadow lost in the darkness. But she couldn't. Elena could never scale a wall or worm her way under a wire fence.

Tess had thought about leaving her in a nearby café or hotel. Somewhere safe. But if Cat and the other women weren't being guarded, maybe Elena could simply explain things to the crew and get the job done without Tess having to strike a single blow. It was a nice idea. And there was a chance it might actually happen. But Tess wouldn't be removing her bulletproof vest anytime soon.

A security barrier blocked the road. They sauntered over to a small, one-story white building with a red roof, light coming from its road-facing window. A big-nosed guard slid open part of the window and peered out from behind a computer monitor.

He and Elena chatted in Polish.

The conversation ended abruptly, when he shook his head and looked back to his monitor while sliding the window shut again.

Tess stuck a roll of notes in the gap to stop the window shutting. With the rest of Michal's money, her emergency stash, and the extra five hundred dollars she'd withdrawn in Krakow airport, she had just shy of a

173

thousand bucks. Not a vast sum. In the West. In the East? The average worker had to toil for months to get such an amount.

The guard looked up to check what was blocking his window. His gaze jumped from Elena to Tess to the money, then back to the monitor.

Without taking his gaze from the monitor, the guard snatched the money and then shut the window.

Elena looked at Tess. Tess shooed her on into to the port.

They scurried in.

Elena pointed to her right. "He said it's docked over there."

Keeping Elena behind her, Tess clung to the shadows of a field of shipping containers as tall as a Manhattan apartment building and as long as a city block. How far back it went, Tess had no idea, but she prayed the container holding Cat was already onboard the ship – they'd never find it on their own if it was still on land.

Skulking through the darkness, Tess crept around the corner of a red container. A ship lurked in the gloom. Emblazoned across its stern was the name: Baltic Empress. They'd found it.

Tess pinned herself to the container as Elena crept around and joined her.

Tess took out her phone. She studied the photos she'd copied from Facebook, so that if she saw the men, she'd recognize them.

Putting her phone away, Tess said, "Stay here. If it's safe and I need you, I'll come for you."

Elena panted for breath and her hands trembled. "But I can help."

"No. You know what I might have to do. I can't worry about you and do that at the same time."

"But—"

"No." Tess gripped her arm. "Listen to me, you have to stay here. The priority is me finding Cat, not me worrying about protecting you. Do you understand?"

"Okay. Yes, you're right."

"You're sure you've got that." Tess couldn't risk being pulled in two directions at once when she needed to focus solely on one objective: rescuing Cat.

Elena nodded forcefully. "Yes, I'm staying here."

Still holding the lady's arm, Tess squeezed it gently. "If I can, I'll bring Cat back to you."

Tess disappeared around the corner, hugging the wall of the container so light from the ship didn't silhouette her out in the open.

Prowling through the darkness, she used her breathing technique to temper her fear and adrenaline levels. It was the only way she would stand a chance of surviving the next ten minutes.

The ship was the biggest vessel she'd ever seen close up, with containers stacked five high on its deck and more in the hold. A gangplank climbed up from the dock to the massive structure in the stern that housed the bridge, crew quarters and such.

On the dockside end of the gangplank, a shape lurked in the darkness. It was a man, because every few seconds, a small glowing red dot moved from being just a few feet off the floor to being higher up – he was smoking. Maybe it was normal to post guards to protect ships from stowaways or the theft of cargo. Or maybe it was confirmation that traffickers were using this ship and they wanted to ensure their precious cargo went undisturbed.

She slunk closer, constantly scanning for threats. She would have to break from the cover of the shadows at some point. When she did, the guard would see her. No question. But in the darkness, would she be able to tell if it was one of the men responsible for taking Cat or not?

She'd have to get close. Have to get close enough to have a good look without being drawn into direct conflict. How could she do that? It was around twenty yards from her shadows to the dockside. No matter how fast she ran, she could never cover so much ground before he saw her and raised the alarm.

Almost drawing level with the ship's stern, she'd have to break cover any moment, but still couldn't identify the guard or figure how to get up the gangplank unseen.

Inspiration flashed a smirk across her face for the briefest of moments.

As if enjoying an afternoon in the park, Tess strolled out of the shadows. Her muscles twitched with nervous energy. Oh God, she hated this moment – those seconds leading up to combat. The uncertainty, the waiting, the doubts. Absolute hell. Only a fool wouldn't be afraid and anxious. Her heart pounded so hard she imagined if someone was standing in front of her, they'd see her chest jerking rhythmically. Only the calm reasoning of her mind pushed her on and prevented her from following her instinct to run far, far away from this hellish place.

As she walked across the dockside access road, light from the ship illuminated her more and more.

She swallowed hard. Game time. Again.

She called out. "Przepraszam."

There was no point in being unseen when being seen could deliver far more satisfying results.

The dark shape at the end of the gangplank turned in her direction and moved toward her. He shouted in Polish.

Tess replied with the single phrase she'd used most often in all her time in the country. "Przepraszam. Er, toaleta? Gdzie?"

A pretty foreigner using broken Polish to ask for the nearest toilet wouldn't raise any flags, but merely imply she was as stupid as she was pretty and had gotten lost. She hoped.

He marched toward her, pointing and spouting Polish. Now in the shade of the ship's hull, however, she still couldn't see if it was one of the men she was hunting. But the shadows did have benefits – no one on the deck could see her without purposefully looking over and shining a light down.

Within striking range, Tess waved as if greeting someone behind him up on the deck. "Oh, dzien dobry, Piotr."

He turned and looked up, presenting his jaw as if begging to be punched on it. Many a professional boxing match was won by a direct shot to the jaw. It was one of the surest ways to get a knockout there was.

Tess smashed a massive right hook into the guy's face.

He twirled around and flopped to the ground face first. He didn't move.

Tess arched an eyebrow. If only all her adversaries went down so easily.

For just a second, she used her phone as a flashlight to check if he was one of the guys she was hunting. He wasn't.

Tess slunk over to the gangplank and crept up the long run of steps which climbed twenty feet or more up the side of the hull. Near the top, she crouched just below deck level and then peeped over.

Deserted.

Time to board the ship.

Time to save Cat.

Time to demand retribution.

Chapter 29

LIKE A GHOST, Tess crept along the gangway. So quiet. So fluid. Almost floating.

She stole her way forward, hugging the metal wall to her right, toward the storage area which consumed the ship from its middle right up to its bow. The ship's skeleton of red-painted steel columns, beams and buttresses dwarfed her.

Hugging the shadows, she stopped and peeled her left glove away from her wrist. Across the skin, she'd noted the container number they'd obtained from the laptop – GDXU 6664219. That was easy – just look for a number beginning 666.

She stepped forward again.

A crewman walked out of an open door right in front of her. He jumped at seeing her.

Before he had time to do anything but gawk at her, she slammed a front kick into his gut.

He doubled over, groaning as though he was going to throw up.

Tess grabbed him around his neck.

Locked her arms.

Squeezed.

Should she cut off his blood supply to render him unconscious, or cut off his air supply to kill him? She tightened her hold.

He flailed and bucked. Raked her steel-clad forearms. Fought for air, his breath rasping and guttural.

But she had him tight.

She squeezed.

Tess would not leave a piece-of-scum trafficker still breathing, but she didn't want to kill an innocent man, either. She hadn't seen him on Facebook so he could be only a crewman.

The man's clawing hands dropped and his weight sank into her arms.

She let him collapse to the green-painted deck. Still breathing. But his mind as black and empty as the night sky.

After hauling him away, she stuffed him into a shadowed alcove created by the ship's infrastructure, where a row of hefty buttresses helped the ship bear the incredible weight of thousands of tons of cargo.

The crewman hidden, Tess prowled onto the open deck toward a wall of containers stacked lengthwise along the vessel, as tall as an apartment building. The wall of yellow, red, blue, white, and brown metal bricks looked like a modernist work of art.

With the ship's lights casting an eerie glow upon the containers, Tess searched for one which had 666 in its unique identifying number. Nothing.

She prayed the container was up here – if she had to venture into the ship's innards to search those stored below deck, it would be impossible to escape detection.

She stalked toward the bow. Along the gangway to her left, a slender handrail overlooked the dock – she wouldn't want to be on a rough sea with only that to save her from falling overboard. To her right were more massive buttresses and beams. And the giant wall of containers which just went on and on.

Men's voices drifted from above and right, somewhere in the mass of containers.

She peered around but found no direct access.

Ahead, a yellow ladder led up to a higher gangway from which it seemed it might be possible to reach the containers. And maybe those voices.

She climbed partway up the ladder, placing her feet softly to avoid a metallic ring signaling those above of her presence.

Peeking onto the next level, she saw a rectangular space about forty feet wide, surrounded on three sides by the enormous metal walls formed from containers – like a clearing in a metal forest. In the far-right corner of the clearing sat two men. They played cards in the glow of a handheld lantern, a couple of beer cans beside them.

Tess's heart leapt as if it were trying to escape through her mouth.

It was them – the men she was hunting.

Mateusz Wojcik, a hefty man with a goatee, and Kuba Jelen, whose goofy teeth made him look cute, but simple. Thank God for Facebook.

She tried to make out the unmistakable outlines of firearms under their clothing, but it was too dark and she was at the wrong angle.

Checking the containers, Tess saw all the ones on the left had only their rears visible, but those on her right had their doors facing into the clearing.

With only the light from the small lantern, and at a poor angle, she struggled to make out the numbers of the containers. She squinted. Strained. No, it was impossible.

Then her jaw dropped.

All the containers were lashed down by two heavy metal rods which ran diagonally across their fronts, forming an X shape. All of them except one. If the containers needed to be lashed to stop them moving when the ship was pummeled by waves, the only reason not to lash one down was so you could still open its doors. Maybe to feed what was inside. She'd finally found Cat!

But how to reach her?

It was impossible to launch a sneak attack on the two guys. In the high-walled metal clearing, there was no way she could reach them without them seeing her. No, she only had one option.

Tess sprang up from the ladder and raced at the men. She had to get to them, before they either raised the alarm or drew weapons.

Kuba shouted in Polish as he struggled to his feet.

Despite his bulk, Mateusz got up quicker. And his hand disappeared under his hoodie. There could be only one reason why – he had a weapon. That made him her first target.

As so many targets had done in the past, Mateusz assumed he had time to pull his weapon before she reached him – after all, she was only a woman so no real threat.

Bounding at him, she leapt into the air. Her flying knee strike smashed into his chest.

A pistol flew from his grasp and skittered across the metal deck while he flew back as if he'd been hit by a wrecking ball. He crashed against the blue container, then crumpled to the deck.

Tess ached to finish him, but in taking out Mateusz, she'd given Kuba time to draw a semiautomatic. He swung it up to aim at her.

But she was already moving. She caught the wrist of his gun arm and swept it away from her just as he pulled the trigger.

A shot blasted into the night.

Still holding his arm with one hand, she drove a palm heel up into his face. As his head jerked back, it sent a spasm through his body and another shot blasted into a red container, then ricocheted away into the blackness with a metallic whine.

Flowing from one move straight into the next, with both hands she cranked an armlock onto his gun arm. Hard. She yanked down with all her might.

Kuba's arm crunched as the joints ripped apart. He wailed and dropped his gun.

Aware Mateusz had clambered up, Tess hammered a back elbow into Kuba's face. Continued turning to smash in a hook. Spun around and crashed in a backfist.

Kuba reeled back against the container.

She spun around, just as Mateusz heaved a massive punch at her head.

Dropping into a crouch, she ducked under his fist and kicked his feet out from under him.

He crunched into the deck and cried out.

She jumped up as Kuba pushed away from the container and hurled himself at her, one arm all but dead at his side.

Tess jumped sideways while hammering a roundhouse kick into his midriff.

Winded, he doubled over, clutching his stomach, gagging for breath.

Tess leapt into the air, then crashed down with her right elbow pointed down at him. It cracked into the back of his neck. He smashed into the deck without making another sound. He would not be getting back up.

She turned.

But Mateusz was stronger than she'd bargained on and was already on his feet.

He heaved a mighty haymaker at her head.

She flung up a block to stop it, but too late – it glanced off her steel forearm guard and clipped the side of her head as she twisted away.

Tess staggered back. If she hadn't been moving away already, she'd have been down and in deep trouble.

He stormed at her. Hurling punches with both fists.

Tess was so well-trained that without even thinking, she analyzed Mateusz's punching. He kept such a steady rhythm, she slipped and ducked each one, while moving around to her left to get the angle she wanted and the opening she knew would come for an easy finish.

He flung another haymaker and stepped around to swing again.

Now she had the angle.

She slipped inside his next punch and powered in a cross to his body, a hook to his temple, and an elbow uppercut to his jaw.

He staggered to the edge of the deck.

Tess thundered a kick into his gut.

He toppled over the handrail and crunched onto the rail of the deck below on his back. His body bent in two the wrong way and then toppled over and smacked into the concrete dockside.

Tess stood still for a moment. Breathed. Let her mind and body calm after the storm.

After a few seconds, she dashed over to the red container that wasn't lashed down with metal rods. On its right door, GDXU 6664219 was stenciled in black.

Tess smiled. She'd found Cat. Found Cat and God only knew how many other poor women.

With no padlock or seal to break, Tess levered up the handle on the first of the two locks barring the right-hand door and swung it around. She then tried to lever the second handle up out of its metal latch. It stuck, metal screeching on metal. She strained to open it.

Whimpering and panicked voices came from inside.

This really was it. She'd really found Cat.

Chapter 30

TESS HIT THE container's handle upward with her palm. Again and again. Each time she hit it, the panicked screams grew louder. Bit by bit, the handle shifted until it was finally free.

The handle finally unlatched, Tess grabbed it to swing it around and free the women.

A shot shattered the stillness.

Tess cried out. As if she'd been hit in the back by a baseball bat, she smashed into the door and then collapsed to the deck.

Elena screamed. A guttural scream drenched in despair.

Pain tearing through Tess's body, she gazed up, lying on her back.

Artur Bartosz, the redheaded man with the seadog face, stared at her. With one hand, he gripped Elena's arm, while his other held a revolver to her head.

He cocked his gun. "On your knees, hands behind your head."

Tears streaming her face, Elena gazed at Tess. "I'm sorry. So sorry."

Wincing with the pain, Tess clambered up to her knees and put her hands behind her head one on top of the other.

Glancing at Kuba's lifeless body, Artur clucked his tongue. He studied Tess. His lined face became even more lined, as if he was deep in thought.

He grimaced with disappointment and shook his head. "You could fetch a good price. But... you're too dangerous. If you killed one of my customers you'd ruin me."

He took his gun away from Elena's head. Aimed it at Tess.

Images flashed into Tess's mind. Images of her home in Manhattan. Of what had happened there. Of who she'd dreamed of finding for so very long, who she'd dreamed of punishing for what felt like her entire life. She'd dedicated the best part of ten years to acquiring the skills to handle any violent situation. But now...

Tess glowered at the gun, at her death.

She was on her knees. A gun aimed at her. Twenty-five feet between her and her attacker. She'd never cover the distance before he pulled the trigger.

She hadn't intended to, but she'd sacrificed the justice she'd dreamed of seeing back home, for a chance to reap justice here. And she'd come close. So very close. It felt good knowing she'd tried. So goddamn good.

Tess smiled a peaceful smile at Elena. Let her know it wasn't her fault. And waited for the bullet that would end her life and her dreams of vengeance.

But Elena lunged. She grabbed Artur's gun hand and sank her teeth into it.

Cursing in Polish, he hurled Elena to the deck. And his gun blasted. Blasted. Blasted!

"No!" Tess screamed, even as her body was leaping up on autopilot, carrying her into battle once more.

She sped across the twenty-five-foot gap at Artur. As he swung his gun around to end her, she leapt into the air.

All in one flowing motion, she caught his gun arm under her left arm and pinned it to her body, clamped her legs around his waist, and hammered her right elbow into his face.

His body jerked under the force of her blow and a shot thundered away into the night sky.

He staggered back and as he smashed into a yellow container, his gun boomed its final shot. But he didn't go down.

He flailed at Tess with his free hand, a punch hammering into her side where his first gunshot had hit her.

She cried out, pain ripping through her torso as if she'd been shot for real. Without meaning to, she relaxed her hold on him.

Both arms now free, Artur grabbed her and crashed her into the container door. He locked his hands around her throat. Squeezed.

Tess's face twisted in pain as she struggled to breathe.

Artur sneered in her face.

He was going to kill her. She had only seconds before he either cut off the blood to her brain or crushed her windpipe. Either way, if she didn't get him off her she was dead. Right here, right now.

Cupping her hands, she flung her arms out wide, then whipped them inwards as hard as she could. Her hands smashed over Artur's ears.

He screeched as his eardrums burst, shooting intense pain straight through his head.

Tess fired an upward elbow into his jaw.

He crunched into the deck with her on top of him.

Tess heaved her right hand far back and let fly with a gigantic punch right into his face. Her steel-gloved fist shattered the bones in his nose. Blood splattered over both of them.

She punched again.

Her fist tore into his face time and again, pulverizing bone, pulping flesh. She pounded, unleashing fury for all of the innocents this monster had abused.

Tess screamed. A scream of rage laced with despair. And she punched and punched and punched and punched.

Finally, gasping for air, exhausted, she stopped and slouched forward.

Artur didn't even look human – his entire face was caved in, like a pumpkin that had been beaten with a mallet.

Panting, Tess rolled off him. Crawled over to Elena. Took the woman's head in her lap.

Blood pooled across the deck from the three holes in Elena's torso.

Tears running down her face, Tess shook her head. "I told you to wait. I told you. You promised you would."

"I-I heard gunshots. I th-thought" – Elena spluttered blood – "thought you needed h-help."

Tess brushed Elena's hair off her forehead. "But I told you to wait. You promised."

Her hand shaking, Elena cupped Tess's cheek. "You're a g-good person, Tess." She spluttered again. "I'd be s-so proud if you w-were my daughter."

Tess choked hearing such words. Her chin quivered. But she struggled to be strong for Elena.

With her hand trembling, Elena pointed toward the container Tess had been opening. Her voice wavered. "Catalina."

Tess gently laid Elena down so she could rest on her side to watch, then pushed to stand. She yelped and clutched her ribs under her right arm. Her bulletproof vest had stopped the bullet from penetrating her body, but it couldn't stop the impact – the pain suggested it had cracked at least one rib. Holding her right side, she lurched over to the container with the lantern.

As Tess heaved open the container door women shrieked inside. Tess shone the lantern in. Engulfed in gloom and eerie shadows, twenty or thirty bedraggled women huddled together at the back of the container.

That was more than they'd had space for in Krakow. Had they stuck more than one woman in a room, or did they have a network of 'hotels' across the country and all the women were shipped en masse?

Beckoning to the women, Tess said, "It's okay, you can come out."

The women exchanged anxious glances.

Tess used the only Polish she knew which might help – please. "Poprosze."

Outside, in the distance, a siren wailed.

Maybe thinking the police were on their way to save them, a blonde woman let go of the brunette next to her and edged toward the door.

Tess coaxed her forward with a wave of her hand. "Poprosze." She stepped to one side so the woman could see the world beyond.

Warily, the blonde tottered out.

Seeing one of their kin escape, others tentatively followed.

Once outside, some women cowered in the clearing's corners, overwhelmed and crying to themselves; some clung to each other, not knowing where to run to; some clambered down the ladder or dropped over the side of the gangway, desperate to be anywhere but there.

"Tess?" called Elena.

Tess looked back.

The blood-soaked lady reached for her.

Tess scampered back. Cradled her again so she could see the women leaving the container. Despite Elena's illness, despite her bullet wounds, she smiled. Smiled like a child at Christmas expecting to find a gift they'd longed for.

The wailing sirens drew closer. Many sirens.

Elena clasped Tess's hand. "Go. I'll w-wait for Cat."

"I'm not leaving you."

"You have to. You'll g-go to p-prison. They won't c-care you saved all these w-women."

"I'm not leaving you."

Woman after woman nervously crept out of their cell. They each gazed up at the moon, at the heavens, and freedom.

"Please, Tess," said Elena. "Leave me."

"Shhh. Watch for Cat."

191

A girl in jeans and naked from the waist up staggered out of the container, her arms clutched across her chest. Then a small woman with a bloody face and a filthy yellow dress hobbled out. And then there was only darkness looming from the container's doorway.

"Catalina?" Elena said, her Christmas smile replaced by a frown.

"I'll find her."

The sirens raced up the dockside. Closer and closer to the ship.

Wincing with each movement, Tess again lurched over to the container. She peered inside. Empty.

Anguish hit Tess as if the bullet had blasted through her vest.

"Oh God, no."

The traffickers didn't only have other 'hotels', they obviously had other women on other ships.

Tess slumped against the door, her legs so wobbly she thought she was going to collapse. She'd sacrificed so much. They'd both sacrificed so much. And this was what they got? She punched the container but immediately flinched and grabbed her side.

Her head hung, she turned to Elena.

The lady had fallen onto her back, eyes staring straight up.

"Elena? Elena!"

Tess dashed to her. Cradled her.

"No." Tess hammered her fist into the deck. Her chest shuddered as she sobbed. "No!"

Somewhere on the ship, she heard police officers shouting, women screaming, panic and commotion.

She had to escape.

Had to get away before they found her.

Tears blurring her vision, Tess glanced around.

She had three choices: leap overboard into the Baltic Sea and swim to safety, praying her broken ribs wouldn't cause her to sink to the seabed; fight her way off the ship through the police, praying there wouldn't be too many trigger-happy heroes; stay with Elena and throw herself at the mercy of the law, praying it would overlook the six men she'd slaughtered and not slam her in a dark, dirty hole for the rest of her life.

Guns drawn, police officers swarmed over the ship, barking commands and herding everyone together. They entered Tess's metal clearing.

Chapter 31

KONRAD NOWAK'S PARTNER pulled their ambulance alongside the two already parked beside the docked container ship. He gaped at all the police cars scattered along the dockside. In all his seventeen years as a paramedic, he'd never seen anything like this.

Climbing out of his ambulance, he shot a quick wave to his colleagues Felix and Kasia as they loaded a woman on a gurney into the back of their ambulance.

Scrambling around to fetch one of his own gurneys, Konrad scanned the ship. Police officers scoured the vessel, their flashlight beams slicing away the night. But cars and officers at a crime scene were nothing new. No, what made this different was the tens of distressed women being corralled together near the stacked containers on the dock.

He and his partner, Hubert, rushed their gurney over to the women, most of whom were huddled on the ground together crying – they looked like a flock of sheep that had been traumatized by a wolf attack. He nodded to the mustachioed police officer guarding them and then helped a blonde woman onto the gurney, her face either dirty or bruised – it was hard to tell in the darkness. They dashed away and put her in the back of the ambulance.

Returned with their second gurney, they delicately lifted a woman up onto it as she drifted in and out of consciousness. They wheeled her to their vehicle too.

While Konrad climbed into the back with their two patients, Hubert leapt into the driver's seat. A moment later, the engine roared, the siren wailed, and away they sped into the night.

In the back of the ambulance, Konrad quickly assessed his two patients. What nightmare they'd endured to end up here he could only guess at – he'd read of the horrors of human trafficking, but never imagined he'd ever see it other than in the movies. But that didn't matter now. The women were safe. All that concerned him was assessing their injuries and seeing they were treated as quickly as possible.

While the blonde woman wailed constantly, the other woman concerned him more because she was covered in blood. However, an initial assessment proved her vitals were strong and that there appeared to be no head trauma and no obvious wound.

Okay, maybe the blonde was the more urgent case – people rarely moaned the way she was without good reason. He moved over to the other patient.

He talked calmly and gently to her, as he flashed a light into her eyes. "Can you tell me your name?"

She flinched at being touched. But her pupils responded correctly to the light.

"Do you know what day it is?"

She whined like a dog that had been left out in the cold but said nothing comprehensible.

He took her pulse. While her heart rate was elevated, which was only to be expected, it was strong and regular. He concluded his initial checks. The woman had no life-threatening injuries but was suffering from shock and extreme dehydration.

After raising her legs, he covered her with an orange blanket, placed a mask over her face to provide oxygen and then administered fluids intravenously.

He turned back to the bloody patient.

The woman lay unconscious. She had blood on her face, on her hands, and on her leather jacket, but he could see no obvious wound. Maybe the blood wasn't hers. However, that needed to be confirmed through a thorough examination.

He unzipped her jacket and then began to cut away her black T-shirt, but stopped. What was that? He felt the strange, stiff material secreted under her clothing. He pulled the cut T-shirt away.

What the hell?

Was that…?

It was. It was a goddamn bulletproof vest.

He looked into the woman's face. Who the hell was she? An undercover cop?

The woman's eyes popped open. Her hand shot out, grabbed him and yanked him down to her.

She clamped her arms around his neck. Squeezed.

He fought, flailing to break free.

He tried to shout for help, but he could barely breathe, barely make a sound. For God's sake, he was trying to help her. Couldn't she see she was in an ambulance?

The inside of the ambulance darkened as his vision tunneled. His brain starved of blood, he was about to black out, but he could do nothing about it. His beautiful Anna flashed into his mind. He wanted to hold her, wanted to—

The ambulance raced toward a sharp left-hand turn onto Jana Pawla II Avenue. Ahead, the shadows of Ronald Reagan Park crawled away into the night. As the vehicle slowed to make the turn, one of its back doors flew open.

Lying half-conscious on the floor of his ambulance, Konrad's eyes flickered open and closed as if seeing the world under a strobe light. Through darkened, blurry vision, he thought he saw the woman leap out of his ambulance, roll across the asphalt, and spring to her feet. Clutching her side, she hobbled toward the park and vanished into the gloom, like a shadow in a dream.

On a straight road again, the ambulance accelerated and shot along the street, siren wailing, lights flashing. Konrad stared at the park as it disappeared into the distance. And then, it too was nothing but a dark memory.

Chapter 32

TESS HEARD ROLLED Rs and a conglomeration of 'sh' and 'ch' sounds that could only be an Eastern European language. She looked at the speaker beside her.

A young man had hoisted his son onto his shoulders to gaze out at Manhattan's skyline, as if the sixty-ninth floor of the Rockefeller Center – the Top of the Rock – wasn't high enough already.

Standing on the observation deck, behind the eight-foot-high protective plexiglass screen, Tess gazed far, far away. In distance and in time.

She sighed.

Was Catalina still out there? Or had her unidentifiable body been laid to rest in an unmarked grave somewhere in Europe, or the Middle East, or even here in the US?

Tess hadn't given up hope of finding her, of honoring the memory of her dear friend Elena, but Krakow and Gdansk felt a lifetime ago.

However, it was always good to be reminded of how all this had begun. Her new life had started that day. By complete accident and to Tess's immense surprise, Elena had changed her life in ways Tess would never have dreamed possible. She'd gone to Asia seeking the tools for revenge but while making her way back home, she had found something very different instead. So very, very different. She'd found purpose.

She hadn't realized it at the time, but the reason she'd become stuck in Europe and hadn't yet claimed her justice was because she simply hadn't been ready. Elena hadn't just provided that answer but had been the catalyst that pushed Tess forward.

Sixty-nine floors below Tess, specks crawled along the streets, each one looking for their own answers, for something to drive their lives forward too. Love, wealth, fame, happiness, achievement, companionship… People looked for their answers in countless places. However, few realized they were all looking for the same thing – purpose, a reason to be. Each one of them deserved the chance to find that which would make them feel complete. And those who lost that chance because they fell victim to someone else's greed deserved something else – justice.

Tess often came up here to watch all these specks and to be reminded of why she did what she did. She hoped she'd never look down from here and feel nothing – no empathy, no sympathy, no… purpose. Other than finding him – which had proved impossible to date, despite all her efforts – this was her sole reason for being. And what better reason could there be than one so noble?

Her cell phone rang. She answered without looking at caller ID. There was no need – only one person ever phoned her.

Tess said, "Hey, Bomb."

"Yo, Tess, I got a location on our boy."

"The rapist or the shooter?" There seemed to be a never-ending line of those who deserved the justice only she could bring.

"The guy whose phone you found – I traced the cell tower ping history."

Tess snatched her black backpack containing all her gear from the concrete floor and turned for the stairs down to the elevators. She walked briskly, with true purpose.

"Great. Send me the details. I'm already moving."

"You got it. Good hunting. Ciao, Tess."

Tess disappeared into the darkness of the stairwell.

A senseless killing demanded payback. And she would claim that payback today. In blood. No argument, prayer, or plea could save them after what they'd done. They would die today. Period.

Who, how, and where she didn't yet know.

But one thing was set in stone – justice would be cold, swift, and brutal. Just another day at the office.

The End.

Continue the adventure. Grab book #2 now using the link below or flip the page for a sneak peek!

Book 02
http://stevenleebooks.com/tz0q
Or order ISBN 978-0-9556525-0-9 from your local bookstore.

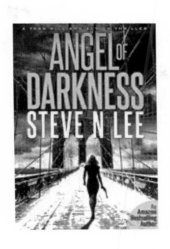

Angel of Darkness

Angel of Darkness Book 02

Angel of Darkness extract

THE RIFLE SCOPE prowled across the park with the dead, emotionless gaze of a great white gliding through the murky depths. From a ledge on the roof of the 150-foot-tall granite tomb, the scope scanned the tree-lined pathways extending from the memorial. The crosshairs skimmed over cold, gray paving stones, stark leafless shrubbery, unlit street lights modeled after nineteenth-century gas lamps, and then...

A young, frizzy-haired woman in a baggy red sweater and black leggings read on a wooden bench in the sharp spring sunshine. Her legs were crossed, the top one moving rhythmically as if tapping to music, yet the area was silent but for the occasional rumble of traffic.

She had no earphones so what was she doing?

Like the caress of a lover's hand, the scope ran along her thigh, over the curve of her knee, and down her slender shin. Finally, it fell upon a baby carriage gently rocking back and forth under the motion of the woman's foot.

He could see the baby clearly – all chubby-faced smiles and sparkling eyes. Lying on its back, it reached upward, fingers grasping and twisting and pointing, as if it was talking in a sign language only it could understand.

Why would any reasonable person bring a child into this godforsaken world?

He stared at the baby. At its cheery face. At its futile gestures. At his scope's crosshairs resting on its forehead.

It would be kinder to end it here. Right now. Why subject the poor thing to seventy-odd years of never-ending struggle, suffering, and disappointment?

He lightly squeezed the trigger. Felt the rifle tense to strike, like a coiled cobra baring its fangs. All he had to do was ease the trigger back one tiny fraction of an inch more, and the child would never have to know the agony of being abandoned by a lover, watching its dreams burn, or burying a loved one.

But his finger relaxed. No, he wasn't taking the baby. Let the mother live with her child's anguish year after year after year. Let her drown in the knowledge that she had brought such sorrow into the world.

The scope prowled on.

A fat man half-walked, half-dragged a brown dachshund along the path to the park that flowed from the memorial down the gentle hillside to the Hudson River. The dog scurried to keep up, but when its stumpy legs failed it, the guy tugged on the leash and hauled it closer.

People. God, how he hated people. The world would be so much better without them.

The crosshairs moved over the man, then the dog, then back to the man.

But which would be kinder? To force the dog to find a new home? Or the man to find a new victim upon whom to express his dissatisfaction with life?

As the scope followed man and beast down the path, it skimmed over something. It stopped and backed up.

A teenager with jeans halfway down his ass spray-painted his tag onto a wall. Even though he was here doing something so mind-numbingly inconsequential, he obviously believed he was special, yet the odds were that he'd never done anything to even hint at that, let alone confirm it. He probably figured people needed to know his name. That he mattered. That he was important. Figured he was the kind of guy who deserved to be recognized and would one day have fame thrust upon him.

The sniper delicately applied pressure to the trigger once more.

He could make the kid so unbelievably famous. In just a matter of hours, everyone in Manhattan would know his name. Hell, the story could even go national. Yep, the kid would be as big as a rock star. Leastways for a day or two.

So, which would this loser prefer? A life of endless mundanity and total anonymity? Or one fleeting moment when his name was on everyone's lips?

Then he heard it.

He gasped. A rush of excited anticipation welled up inside him and exploded, flooding his body with the closest thing to joy he could remember.

Forsaking the graffiti artist, he swung the telescoping lens around so quickly that the image was just a muddy blur. He stopped and studied the new view only to find that he'd become lost among the rooftops of Harlem. In his haste, he'd overshot the target.

He drew a deep, steadying breath.

Calmness. Stillness. Patience. Those were the secrets to a successful kill shot.

As his excitement waned, he let the scope pan slowly back in the direction of the park.

And all the while, church bells pealed announcing the happy union of two people who were so desperately in love they needed a piece of paper to prove it.

Finally, the crosshairs found Riverside Church's gigantic stone tower, so gigantic it was more like a mini-skyscraper than a humble bell tower. The scope crawled down, down, down the stone wall, interrupted intermittently by the bare branches of the trees lining one of the pathways in between him and it.

Eventually, it came to the crowd of impeccably dressed people gathered on the sidewalk. While talking among themselves, few could tear their gaze away from the church entrance, where stone steps led up to heavy wooden doors decorated with black wrought iron curls and swirls.

Moments later, a chisel-jawed hunk in a dark suit and a black woman with a fashion-magazine-cover figure strolled out hand in hand. The crowd cheered and hurled handfuls of rice.

The two lovers stood on the entrance's top step obviously adoring being showered with such attention. Cameras clicked. Flashes flashed. Rice rained.

The scope crawled over the bridegroom. A typical white, entitled asshole. Born into money. Everything handed to him on a plate. The only tangible contribution he'd ever make to the world would be to bring more entitled mouths into it. Just what the world needed.

The crosshairs moved sideways.

And there she was - the ever-loving, ever-fawning, two-faced, gold-digging whore. How many men had she had to bang before she finally landed today's soulmate? Twenty? Fifty? A hundred?

In turn, the scope magnified each of their faces. Each of their sickeningly happy, grinning faces.

Hatred quickened his breath and his heart hammered. His muscles tensed so much that he involuntarily gripped the rifle harder. Too hard.

The weapon wobbled as his contempt shook his sharpshooting expertise. So much so that the target disappeared from his scope, and all he saw was part of the tower once more.

He cursed under his breath and dragged a hand up over his brow and back over his short-cropped graying hair. At this distance, gravity would force a projectile to travel in an arc, so to make the perfect kill shot, allowances had to be made for that when aiming. As if that didn't make the shot complicated enough, temperature, altitude, and humidity had to be considered, too. But those weren't the biggest threats. No, that was down to the wind - over a long distance, the tiniest of gusts could alter a bullet's trajectory and literally blow it off course. Being just a hair's breadth off with his calculations could mean being inches off target at the point of impact. He'd only get one clean shot at this, so he couldn't afford to miss. That meant he had to be statue-still.

He closed his eyes. Breathing slowly and deeply, he forced his hatred and anger down. Forced his body to calm. Blanked everything except himself, his weapon, and his target. Gradually, his hands steadied and the scene through the scope was once more still.

Again, the grinning faces taunted him.

So, should he try to take both of them? Or settle for just one?

That was a tough call.

Luckily, he had time to enjoy the spectacle and to make his decision. Or did he? What if they planned on disappearing into the park to have photos taken, or being whisked away to a party by the black limousine waiting at the curb?

No, there was nothing to be gained from waiting.

He took aim, placing the crosshairs at the very top of the target's forehead to allow for drop, so gravity would work in his favor and not against him.

Gently squeezing the trigger just a fraction, he savored the moment as the weapon ached to be unleashed.

He smirked. Almost done.

Chapter 02

Alone in Marlowe's Grounds, Tess Williams shook her head, sitting at a round table with a white vase in the center holding a plastic pink orchid.

What was wrong with the world? Well, not the world. The world was doing just fine. No, it was people. What the hell was wrong with people?

Cradling her coffee, she closed her blue eyes and drew a deep, relaxing breath in through her nose. She held it, and then let it out slowly through her mouth. She opened her eyes again. The world was just as she'd left it. Sadly.

The aroma of fresh Javan coffee wafted up from her cup. She stared at the wisps of steam for a moment, then looked back over the heads of the customers at the coffee shop's counter and to the wall-mounted television which featured breaking news from Riverside Church, Morningside Heights. The couple couldn't have picked a more beautiful spring morning for a wedding. Nor a more beautiful church. Couldn't fault them there. They must have figured it would be a perfect day.

The woman reporter tried to look concerned, but all Chanel and attitude, was clearly ecstatic at having landed such a high-profile story. She gestured over the police cordon to the church, where a forensics team scoured the steps and detectives spoke with traumatized wedding guests.

She said, "As you can see, Peter, the police have sealed off the area and are investigating what is yet another truly heinous shooting. The third in just seven days."

In the studio, so well-groomed he looked like a waxwork model, the news anchor, Peter, said, "And I believe Channel 7 has obtained some exclusive footage, isn't that right?"

"Yes, Peter. It reveals the full horror of what happened here today."

Peter looked directly into camera. "Sensitive viewers might wish to look away for a moment as this footage contains some disturbing images."

A shaky handheld video appeared with black bars down either side because the cell phone owner hadn't turned the device sideways to film in landscape mode.

While church bells pealed, a guy in a gray Armani suit and a skinny black woman in a white gown that must have cost as much as a small car stood before the aged wooden doors of Riverside Church.

A crowd of well-wishers cheered and showered them with rice.

The male phone owner shouted, "Give her a kiss."

The groom kissed his new wife and then grinned at the crowd as people clapped.

A rifle shot blasted.

The bride crashed backwards into the church doors. Flesh bursting from where her right eye had been. Blood spattering her wedding gown. So bright, so shockingly red against such virginal white.

For a micro-second, the world froze. Then, after the initial moment of the remarkable stillness that shock always brings, panic erupted.

For a few seconds, the picture was a blur of running, the sound a cacophony of screaming.

The phone owner scurried over to the cover of a limousine parked outside the church. Unbelievably, he continued filming and panned his phone across the chaos.

A woman in a long lemon dress dragged her screaming daughter away, but her dress knotted around her legs. She crashed to the sidewalk. Scrambling up, she lifted the girl with one hand, her dress with the other, and then ran for the sanctuary of the church.

Clutching two wailing children to his chest, a young guy sprinted into the road, a woman trailing alongside. A black car blared its horn and swerved. The family didn't even look, but just shot for the cover of the trees of Riverside Park.

All around, guests grappled with each other to flee the carnage.

The camera owner's voice shook as he spoke. "Oh, God. I—I don't know what's happening... It's like... I don't know... someone's shooting and... Oh, God..." He gasped. "Oh, no... Oh, God, no... Angelique."

On the church steps, the groom sat on the unforgiving stone beside his wife. He pulled her lifeless, blood-drenched body to him.

In the background, globs of blood, chunks of brain, and shards of skull slid down the dark church doors like some grotesque artwork by one of the inmates in an institution for the criminally insane.

An older bald man knelt beside him. He looked at all those running for shelter, running to distance themselves from the happy couple whose perfect day they'd been so eager to share.

The man shouted, "Get an ambulance! For God's sake, get an ambulance."

The groom cradled Angelique and sobbed. Tears ran down his cheeks as blood ran into the gutter.

The news anchor reappeared. "That truly is shocking, Janice. And again, ladies and gentlemen, that's a Channel 7 exclusive. As you know, we always strive to be the first to bring you the news that matters. So, Janice, what's the official response to the incident? Do the police suspect it's the work of the Pool Cleaner?"

"Well, Peter, while it's way too early to speculate, it does fit the profile, the incident involving a Caucasian male and an African American female, so initial indications do indeed point to another Pool Cleaner killing, yes. Though there hasn't yet been official confirmation, I'm sure it won't be long in coming."

Tess hung her head. It just never stopped. So she could never stop.

She took a last gulp of her coffee, then shutdown her tablet and stuffed it into her black backpack. Her article on gang violence in Little Russia would have to wait. Another story had grabbed the headlines. A story she'd hoped she'd only ever see reported and never have to become a part of. But like that was ever going to have happened.

She strode toward the door. While most people shuffled or loped or lumbered or slouched, Tess flowed, her gait effortless, gliding, like an exquisite Swiss timepiece, each part precision engineered to interact perfectly with the next.

With slabs of gray cloud gnawing away the blue sky, the sharp spring air bit like a starving dog at the boy teasing it. Tess zipped up her black leather jacket as she exited the coffee shop and emerged onto Broadway.

When the average person thought of Broadway, they pictured the razzmatazz of theater shows, seeing famous actors in the flesh, and the excitement of Times Square. Few people realized that the vast proportion of this world-famous landmark was nothing but an ordinary city street, like countless other city streets across the US. Burger joints, delis, banks, cafés, grocery stores... Broadway ran the length of Manhattan and then continued on for miles. To most New Yorkers, Broadway was merely another street. Nothing exotic. Merely functional.

Amid the honking and growling traffic, a yellow cab pulled up to the curb in front of Tess. A fat guy in a gray overcoat struggled out and then waddled down the sidewalk. Within seconds, he became just another nondescript face in the crowd that people passed without even noticing. In a city with a population of eight million, it was easy to disappear, to be but a blur in the shadows of the most vibrant place on Earth.

211

Tess strode on, scanning the street ahead and registering the situation on autopilot. The usual assortment of pedestrians cluttered the sidewalk, none appearing to deserve more than a cursory glance. A traffic camera clung to a metal pole at the end of the block, surveilling the junction, but if she hugged the building to her left as she approached, she'd be out of its line of sight. Heading north, the tail end of a police cruiser disappeared into the traffic, its distance and direction making it of little consequence. No uniforms patrolled either sidewalk.

Minimal threat.

Not that anyone was looking for her. Especially not the police. Well... they were, they just didn't know it. Because of the expertise with which Tess masked her activities, New York's finest were looking for multiple suspects in connection to a mounting number of unsolved homicide cases. They did not appreciate that all those crimes were the sole responsibility of just one person – her. On the contrary, thanks to the public persona she'd established, more than a few law enforcement officers would swear under oath that she was a model citizen. That persona took a considerable amount of work to maintain, but was worth the effort.

She checked the angle of the traffic camera to ensure it hadn't been altered since the last time she'd passed this way. It hadn't.

No, no one was looking for her. However, in her line of work, she found it best to keep her movements as under-the-radar as possible.

She slunk closer to the wall, to ensure she was outside the range of the camera when she neared it.

Then she saw it.

She sighed. The Pool Cleaner crime scene was active right now. It was imperative she get there as soon as possible, not least to try to catch the detective she'd seen interviewing people in the background on the news broadcast. But...

Not yet within range of the camera, Tess meandered back toward the curb to get the angle she needed. As she passed a newsstand on her right, she looked left. The reflection in the first-floor wall of glass of the Michenner Building revealed a newsstand plastered with newspapers and magazines, a bearded man peering out from inside, and...

Under her breath, she said, "Goddamnit."

She didn't need this now, but could she really sail on by if something was going down?

***

"A good fast-paced read with a fabulous female lead."
5 stars – Julie Elizabeth Powell

"Great plot with plenty of twists."
5 stars – John Ellis

"Great stuff. Jack Reacher meets Girl with the dragon tattoo."
5 stars – *Linn Caroleo*

Use this link to get *Angel of Darkness* (book 02):
http://stevenleebooks.com/tz0q
Or order ISBN 978-0-9556525-0-9 from your local bookstore.

Free Library of Books

Thank you for reading *Kill Switch*. To show my appreciation of my readers, I wrote a second series of books exclusively for you – each *Angel of Darkness* book has its own *Black File*, so there's a free library for you to collect and enjoy (books you cannot get anywhere else).

Start Your FREE Library with *Black File 01*.
http://www.stevenleebooks.com/xbu5

This also entitles you to get my VIP readers newsletter every month, with some combination of:

- news about my books
- special deals/freebies from me or my writer friends
- opportunities to help choose book titles and covers
- anecdotes about the writing life, or just life itself
- behind-the-scenes peeks at what's in the works.

Make Your Opinion Count

Do you know that less than 1% of readers leave reviews?

It is unbelievably difficult for an emerging writer to reach a wider audience, so will you help me by sharing how much you enjoyed this book in a short review, please? I'll be ever so grateful.

Don't follow the 99% – stand out from the crowd with just a few clicks!

Thank you,

Steve

Copy the link to post your review
http://stevenleebooks.com/awwi

Angel of Darkness Series

Book 01 – Kill Switch

This Amazon #1 Best Seller explodes with pulse-pounding action and heart-stopping thrills, as Tess Williams rampages across Eastern Europe in pursuit of a gang of sadistic kidnappers.

Book 02 – Angel of Darkness

Set in Manhattan, Tess hunts a merciless killer on a mission from God in a story bursting with high-octane action and nail-biting suspense.

Book 03 – Blood Justice

Blood Justice erupts with the intrigue, betrayal and red-hot action surrounding a senseless murder. Thrust into the deadly world of crime lords and guns-for-hire, only Tess can unveil the killer in this gripping action-fest.

Book 04 – Midnight Burn

An unstoppable killing-machine, Tess demands justice for crimes, whatever the cost. But even 'unstoppable' machines have weaknesses. Discover Tess's as she hunts a young woman's fiendish killer.

Book 05 – Mourning Scars

Crammed with edge-of-your-seat action, suspense, and vengeance, this adventure slams Tess into the heart of a gang shooting and reveals the nightmare that drove her to become a justice-hungry killer.

Book 06 – Predator Mine

Bursting with nerve-shredding intrigue, this page-turner plunges Tess into the darkest of crimes. And dark crimes deserve dark justice. Discover just how dark a hero can be when Tess hunts a child killer.

Book 07 – Nightmare's Rage

If someone killed somebody you loved, how far would you go to get justice? How dark would be too dark? How violent too violent? Vengeance-driven Tess is about to find out in an electrifying action extravaganza.

Book 08 – Shanghai Fury

Tess Williams is a killer. Cold. Brutal. Unstoppable. In a white-knuckle tale of murder, mayhem, and betrayal, discover how her story begins, how an innocent victim becomes a merciless killing-machine.

Book 09 – Black Dawn

Everything ends. Including a life of pain, hardship, and violence. Tess has sacrificed endlessly to protect the innocent by hunting those that prey upon them. Now, it's time to build a new life for herself. But a news report changes everything.

Book 10 – Die Forever

A brutal gang is terrorizing NYC. Tess's hunt takes her to one of the deadliest places on the planet, for one of her deadliest battles. How will she get out alive?

About Steve N. Lee

Steve lives in Yorkshire, in the north of England, with his partner Ania and two cats who adopted them.

Picture rugged, untamed moorland with Cathy running into Heathcliff's arms – that's Yorkshire! Well, without the running. (Picture jet-black bundles of fur – that's their cats.)

He's studied a number of martial arts, is a certified SCUBA diver, and speaks 10 languages enough to get by. And he loves bacon sandwiches smothered in brown sauce.

Use the link below to learn more – some of it true, some of it almost true, and some of it, well, who really knows? Why not decide for yourself?

http://stevenleebooks.com/a5w5

Made in the USA
Columbia, SC
07 March 2021

34027804R00131